Face into the Wind

Face into the Wind

Rosalind Gill

Stories

Library and Archives Canada Cataloguing in Publication

Title: Face into the wind : stories / Rosalind Gill.

Names: Gill, Rosalind (Rosalind M.), author.

Identifiers: Canadiana (print) 20230510558 |
Canadiana (ebook) 20230510566 |

ISBN 9781771617284 (softcover) | ISBN 9781771617291 (PDF) |
ISBN 9781771617307 (EPUB) | ISBN 9781771617314 (Kindle)

Classification: LCC PS8613.I4525 F33 2023 | DDC C813/.6—dc23

Published by Mosaic Press, Oakville, Ontario, Canada, 2023.

MOSAIC PRESS, Publishers
www.Mosaic-Press.com
Copyright © Rosalind Gill 2023

MOSAIC PRESS
1252 Speers Road, Units 1 & 2, Oakville, Ontario, L6L 5N9
(905) 825-2130 • info@mosaic-press.com • www.mosaic-press.com

For my husband, Peter

For my husband

Table of Contents

Acknowledgements

Many thanks to all those who helped me create this book: Anne Budgell, Stevie Cameron, Gail Collins, Miriam Edelson, Amy Gottlieb, Jeannie Weerasinghe, Beth Kaplan, Christine Klein-Lataud, Heidi Mckenzie, Christina Parker, Piera Savage, Judy Steed, Leslie Vyrenhoek, b.h. yael, and to my husband Peter and my wonderful family and friends for their love and support.

Hoist Your Sails and Run

My heart pounding, I ran down the laneway by the Kelly house and hid under their high back steps. It smelled dank in there, earthy and moldy. And it was scary. I could sense spiders watching me from dark corners and worms crawling silently across the damp ground. But I stayed put in my hiding place.

A few minutes later, I heard the slap of feet as a couple of other kids came running down the lane. Through the latticework covering, I could see that it was Patsy Danson and her brother Mickey. They were out of breath, arguing about where to look for me.

"Come on, I bet she's gone into the field," said Mickey, shoving his little sister ahead in that brutish way of his. And off they went, across the garden and through the hole in the fence.

I was glad enough to see them go off. Mickey was a real toughie. He'd pushed me aside earlier when the Hoist Your Sails crew was being assembled. "Don't let her play, she's only seven, too little."

But Jimmy Kelly, a softer and much nicer boy, had come to my rescue. "Ah! come on, Mick b'y. Everyone gets to play hide and seek—boys, girls, little ones, older ones. Don't be so mean."

Thinking back on it now, Mickey Danson was right—I was too young to be playing Hoist Your Sails, especially with those rough and tumble kids. Despite the passing of the years, I can still picture them, quick and lively, with their tousled hair and scruffy shoes.

I stayed in my hiding place for what seemed like an eternity. No one else came down the lane, but I could hear excited kids running and calling out to each other out on the street. The evening light was waning, and the air was getting cold when I finally came out. What now? I didn't quite understand how the game worked. If no one found me, did I win?

As I slipped out from behind the steps, the back door of the Kelly house squeaked open. Still in hiding mode, I ducked behind the garbage cans and peeked at the adults in the doorway. It was Jimmy Kelly's mother—and to my breathless surprise, my own father. Mrs. Kelly was smiling. Her flouncy sleeveless dress displayed the tan on her freckly arms. But Daddy—what was he doing there in the doorway with her, dressed in his work suit?

He muttered something, close in Mrs. Kelly's ear, patted her bum and scurried down the rickety steps. Mrs. Kelly went back inside and closed the door.

I waited till he was out of sight before going up the lane. Then, in the setting sun, I raced down the street to my house. Mom was in the doorway. "Where have you been, my child?" She was agitated and a little cross, as she had been a lot lately. "I told you not to be playing with those ruffians. They've been racing around the neighbourhood all evening."

Over her shoulder, I could see Dad, taking his jacket off. "Hi lovie," he called out, forcing a smile. "Better get in the house now, getting late."

I stepped inside, avoiding Dad's eyes. I was confused about what I'd seen over at the Kellys but I knew I'd come upon something important. My instinct was to tuck the secret away.

Such was the world of tucked away secrets I grew up in, sensing that some things were taboo, watching for cues from adults about what could be revealed and what had to remain under tabs. My little stomach churned with nervosity as I learned to play that game, but learn I did, and I quickly became adept at it.

At the next round of Hoist Your Sails, no one objected to me, but when the various hiding groups were formed, I was not included. Left to my own devices, I returned to the Kellys' back steps, not so much to hide as to snoop. I had a long wait, watching a spider tend to her web in that dank hiding place. Then I heard the back door open. It was Mrs. Kelly. She came down the stairs, went into the back yard and hung a bra on the line. It dangled there boldly, all by itself. When my mother put the washing out, she modestly bunched the underwear between the towels so as not to display her "smalls," as she called them. Yet another detail from that long-ago summer that's still crystal clear in my mind: Mrs. Kelly's emblematic lace bra hanging brazenly from the clothesline.

I took a good look at her, comparing her to my mother. She was slim like Mom, but not as neat. Her strawberry blond hair was soft and unkempt, falling to her shoulders, and her crumpled blouse had a button missing. My mom's hair, cut in a short crop, was always combed and in place. And she spent copious hours ironing, so no blouse went unpressed in our household. No buttons loose or missing, either.

In a moment of boldness, I jumped out from behind the steps, stood in the garden as if I'd just arrived and said, "Hello Mrs. Kelly, is Jimmy here? We're playing Hoist Your Sails and I'm looking for him."

She turned and gave me a radiant smile. "No, my darling, he'd be off hiding somewhere else. Did they leave you all alone? You're a bit young for this, aren't you?" She was all kindness. And so pretty. Luscious temptation for my beleaguered dad, I now realize. "I'm just going into the house. Can I get you a cookie?" she asked in the softest of voices.

Mom's voice rang in my ears: "Never accept food from the neighbours. Who knows what kind of dirt they have in their kitchens!" But I went ahead and emitted a little "I don't care" (that's how kids said "yes please" in those days).

We sat on the steps, munching Purity gingersnaps straight out of the package. Mrs. Kelly smelled of "Evening in Paris" cologne. Mommy had a bottle of that too, but only wore it on special occasions. "Is your daddy home tonight?" asked Mrs. Kelly, her amber eyes twinkling.

Butterflies flitted in my stomach.

"No, he's gone to work. Night shift." Two doors away, I could hear my mother calling out to me. "Time to get in the house, Jeannette. Come straight home now, darling."

I stood up, cookie in hand, and shut the moment down. "I better go, my mommy's calling."

Daddy was home—I'd lied to Mrs. Kelly. When I came into the house, wiping crumbs off my mouth, my parents were having one of their arguments. Those moments had become part of the landscape for me, a rough landscape, for sure. Mom was at the ironing board pressing her new tablecloth. She raised her voice sharply, making me cringe. "This can't go on, Bob, you've got to ask for a raise, so we can get a better house."

I loved our little blue clapboard bungalow. For me, it had a dollhouse quality to it, compact, with square-paned windows and an arched roof like you see in storybooks. But Mom complained about it being cramped and drafty. Dad teased her, as he often did. "Oh, Mrs. is not from the West End, wants to go back to the big Victorian mansions in the East End. Sure, it's all fog down there. At least we get a bit of summer up here." Sometimes Mom went along with his teasing. We'd all laugh, and my churning little belly would go nice and smooth as I felt the unity of the three of us in our fairy-tale house.

But that night Mom was in no joking mood. She folded the white tablecloth, aligning the corners perfectly. "Don't be gettin' on with your charm tonight, Bob. I'm serious. I simply don't like the element on this street. You don't care if we live alongside the dregs of society, but I certainly do."

After the cookie on the steps with Mrs. Kelly, I started hanging around the Kelly house, drawn to her and her cheerful, soft manner and curious about her secret connection with my daddy.

I'd walk past the windows with their dusty curtains, watching to see who was coming and going.

Jimmy Kelly saw me on the sidewalk and called out, beckoning me into the garden. "Want to play allies?" Jimmy was a special boy. No shoving and pushing with him. And he didn't mind playing with girls, even little ones like me, although he was almost nine. Jimmy loved to talk. He adored his mother and boasted of the good times he had with her, playing cards and watching "I Love Lucy" on TV. He even told me his family secrets. "Daddy works on the trains. You should see him in his uniform. But he's away a lot. Then when he comes home, he's tired. Mom says he's no fun."

I listened to his stories, noticing the perplexed, sad look on his face when he mentioned his dad: but already a good keeper of secrets, I didn't offer any stories about my own "no fun" household.

Before long, Jimmy and I ventured out of the garden and started playing in the little woods at the end of the field. Time was magic with Jimmy. Slipping through the trees like fairies, we giggled and chatted. Two only children with no siblings, we gave each other rich and wondrous company. The little copse we played in became a gigantic forest where we invented worlds. Unlike other boys, Jimmy didn't mind playing "house"—he'd be the kind daddy and me the protective mommy, nurturing our imagined children—rocks, twigs, ferns, and daisies, all lined up and brought to life by our combined fantasy. No arguments, no lies, just happy families.

Another round of Hoist Your Sails. This time I hoped to team up in a hiding place with Jimmy, but his dad had taken him around the bay to visit his grandparents in Avondale. As the kids took off to their hiding places, I deftly tagged along with two older boys from the far end of the street and an older girl called Tomasina who sometimes visited her aunt a few doors down from us. They were going to hide out behind the little falling-down shed where Mr. Patrick did his carpentry. The Patricks lived next door to the Kellys and to get to their backyard, we had to go down the Kellys' laneway. Going down the lane, I saw a shadow of someone moving in the Kellys' kitchen window. I stepped back and took another look. Sure enough, it was my dad—all I could see was his arm, but his hairy wrist and Timex watch were a dead giveaway. Suddenly, he was full-faced in the window, trying to shimmy it up, to let in air in the muggy night. The window was stuck, and he had to rattle it hard, and as he did so, he caught sight of me.

His eyes widened and his jaw dropped as he let go of the half-opened window. It shut with a bang. To this day, I can still hear that sound. It was a pivotal moment—that gaping look on my dad's face made me realize, on some level, that he was up to no good.

In a panic, I raced to catch up with the other kids, who were already behind the Patricks' shed. The two boys were toughies for sure, but mercifully, they ignored me. First, they devoted themselves to pulling Tomasina's braids and the straps on her sundress, and then they started ripping a rotten board off the back of the shed so they could see inside. Someone had told them Mr. Patrick hid old "girlie" magazines in there. Watching them get up to their shenanigans, all I could think of was my dad. I had dread in my stomach. He knew that I knew. Did that mean I was in trouble? Or was he in trouble?

This time, the wait in the hiding place was short-lived. Mr. Patrick came striding through the garden, red in the face with fury, and rousted us out. "I'll tell your parents you were here destroying my property," he roared. This only deepened the pit of anxiety opening up in me.

As I headed home, I thought of Mom, unaware that Dad was just down the street with Mrs. Kelly. Before going into the house, I went into the field and picked her a bunch of blue harebells and bright yellow butter-and-eggs.

She was in the living room, flipping through the *Readers Digest* and happily took the flowers. "Oh, what a pretty bouquet."

But despite my attempt to smooth things over, she sensed there was something wrong. "What's bothering you, darling? Your colour is off."

Again, I was quick to lie. "Oh, I don't like the boys who play Hoist your Sails," I said, falling into her lap. She felt like a real haven. Reliable, smelling of nice clean Lux soap and bound to be herself. No surprises.

Shortly afterward, Dad came in, supposedly from work. I was tucked away in bed but wide awake. I seem to remember being awake a lot in those summer nights, agitated by the increasing conflict between my mom and dad and the secret I was sitting on.

The bedroom door opened, letting in a shaft of light. Dad slipped in and sat on the bed. I stirred.

"I just wanted to say, darlin', don't worry about earlier this evening," he said, softly. "I was just helping Mrs. Kelly with her new stove." His voice went to a whisper. "But don't be telling your mother you saw me there—you know she doesn't like the neighbours."

I could barely see his face in the shadowy room, but it seemed to be contorted by an expression I had never seen before. Usually, I liked it when Dad and I had our own little moments together, like the times he comforted me when Mom was being too strict—but this time, it didn't feel right.

Jimmy Kelly's ninth birthday party. Mom dressed me up in a crinoline dress and set my hair in ringlets. I squirmed and complained as she took the papers out. "I hate ringlets; they make me look silly."

"We've got to get you done up for the party, Jenny—though I must say, the Kellys don't look like the type to stand on much ceremony."

Mom insisted on taking me by the hand to the birthday party. Going into Dad's secret territory with her made me feel suddenly uncomfortable, and I tripped and fell on the Kellys' steps. Mom pulled me up and brushed me off. "For heaven's sake, don't go getting dirt on your good dress." We pushed the Kellys' unlatched door open and were blown back by the din of children shouting and running around. Mom stood formally in the doorway, bristling with disapproval.

Mrs. Kelly called out over the racket, "Come on in, if you can get in!"

"Oh, thank you, but no," said Mom, stepping back, "I have a meeting at the church. Just came to greet the birthday boy."

She summoned up a smile. "Happy Birthday, Jimmy, and thank you for inviting Jeanette to your party." She turned to me, fixing an errant ringlet. "Have fun and behave yourself, now, Jenny." And off she went.

It took me a few minutes to shake off the nervosity of seeing my mom at the Kelly house. It seemed like Dad's big lie was floating in the very air, and I was scared she might have seen it.

Most of the kids at Jimmy's party were the raggle-taggle Hoist Your Sails crew. In my stiff dress and ringlets, I stayed by the party table, drinking syrup out of a paper cup with a cowboy print to match the birthday tablecloth. There was another little girl there, pinned against the wall, looking shy and out of place. I knew it was Jimmy's cousin from Avondale, a bay girl overwhelmed by the brazen townies. I picked up a birthday blower from the table and offered it to her. Before long we were playing in our own quiet way.

Mrs. Kelly came over and put her arm around me. "You're a lovely girl, Jeanette. You must come in and visit more often." Jimmy came to me as well, leaving the crew to their antics. Mrs. Kelly put her arm around him too and he beamed. He was clearly his mommy's boy and even had the strawberry blond hair and freckles to prove it.

When it came time to blow out the candles on the cake, a tall skinny man appeared in the kitchen door. He looked pale, ghost-like. "This is my dad," said Jimmy, casting his eyes down. Mr. Kelly hardly responded.

After that, I spent more time at the Kellys' house. Mrs. Kelly never mentioned my dad to me again. But she took delight in spoiling Jimmy and me, laughing and joking with us, letting us fill our bellies with all the cookies we wanted. I was constantly comparing their home with my own, where cookies (always homemade) were limited because Mom had to keep some back for events at the church. And Mrs. Kelly seemed so carefree, even a little wild, dancing away in the kitchen to the "Top Ten" on the radio. So unlike my mom who, as my dad said, "always had a pot of worry on the stove."

Cultivating my own little lie of omission, I was careful not to tell Mom about my visits to the Kellys. For sure she wouldn't approve.

Mrs. Pitt from next door was chatting to Mom over the back fence. "We don't be seeing much of your husband these days," she probed.

Mom answered smoothly. "Oh, Bob's working overtime at the paper."

Mrs. Pitt folded her arms across her chest, glancing in the direction of the Kelly house. "That's a lot of hours he's clocking in!"

I hid behind my mother, in case Mrs. Pitt could somehow see the truth of the matter on my face.

Mom explained further, as if proud of her husband's importance. "Bob has to be there when they put the paper to print late at night."

But inside our little bungalow, there was more than one row about Dad's absences. "I know you want to get ahead but you're always at work, Bob. Can't someone spell you? *The Daily News* must have the resources to let you spend more time with your family. Even the neighbours are noticing that you're not around much."

Dad was busy reading *The Evening Telegram*, the rival newspaper. My memory of him in those arguments with Mom is that he always remained unfazed by the depth of her frustration.

"It's just that right now, there's a lot of big news, Phyllis. News releases on the Korean War keep coming in off the wire. And there's endless debate on the city council about the new housing. Now that Canadian money is flowing in, there's a big building boom in St. John's. I need to be on the job."

By then, I had a whole new fix on the tension between my parents. I knew more about the real picture than my mom did. The day before, Jimmy and I had turned up unexpectedly at the Kellys, having curtailed our trip to the woods because of rain. Mrs. Kelly called out faintly from the bedroom, "I'll be out in a minute." Then she came into the kitchen, her blouse not tucked in and no shoes on. "I s'pose you two explorers will be wantin' a snack now," she said in her generous way.

I heard coughing from the bedroom—my dad's smoker's cough. Mrs. Kelly turned the radio on loud. I remember the song that came blasting out: "Secret Love" by Doris Day. I looked over at Jimmy, but he was playing with his cowboy rope and didn't seem to notice anything. I'd never breathed a word to him about my dad and his mom. He seemed blissfully unaware, so I acted as if I hadn't heard the coughing.

Mrs. Kelly sent us out to the shed with our cookies so she could "clean the kitchen floor." As I sat out there with Jimmy, rain tapping on the roof, an unformed thought was hanging around in the back of my little-girl's mind—here we were, my dad and I, both hanging out at the Kellys' house. And mixed into the swirl of emotions I had about it all was a growing resentment that I had to share my own secret place with him.

A late August day. Jimmy was off in Avondale again. At a loss for what to do, I was just thinking about visiting Mrs. Kelly and got to the top of the laneway when I saw my dad slipping into her garden from the field and heading for her kitchen door. I felt mad and vengeful. Why should he go there and not me? I stewed about it all afternoon.

At supper time, Mom said it would be just the two of us, as Dad had to work. I was almost tempted to blurt out "Daddy's over to Mrs. Kelly's" but I'd become used to holding the secret tightly to myself, especially since the lie had become a tangled web that included my own sneaking around behind Mom's back.

Over supper, I was cross and refused to eat the salt fish she'd prepared. "I hate that stuff, and you're always making it. Why can't we have chicken?"

Mom was in a bad mood too. "That's enough of your mouth, child. I've no time for that nonsense this evening."

She was distraught because the ceiling light in the kitchen wouldn't come on, and the landlord had not turned up to fix it. After supper, she moved a chair into the middle of the kitchen. "I'm going to get up and see what I can do. Maybe it's just the bulb." While she was up there fiddling, the chair wobbled, and she came crashing down.

"Oh, I've hurt my arm," she screamed. She sat on the floor, in pain, holding her wrist. I could see that the bone was hanging at an odd angle. And her face had gone pale.

"I'll have to go to Emergency and have it seen to," she moaned. "Go next door and ask Mr. Pitt if he'll drive us to the hospital."

I raced outside and headed for the Pitts' house, but something made me stop and pause on the sidewalk for a second. To this day, I'm not sure if it was spiteful anger at my father or loyalty to my injured mother that made me turn on my heels and run directly in the opposite direction to Mrs. Kelly's. As I banged on the back door, through the kitchen window I could see Dad sitting at the table, cheerfully chatting away, his mouth moving, saying words I couldn't hear. The sight of him gave me a sharp pang of jealousy that he should find happiness away from me and Mom.

Mrs. Kelly opened the door and I yelled, "Mommy had an accident—she broke her arm." Dad came rushing out, putting his jacket on. Luckily, that day he was driving *The Daily News* van and was able to take us straight to the hospital. "Thank God you came home early, Bob," said Mommy, holding her wrist.

At the hospital, we had a long wait while a cast was put on. Dad sat next to me, hanging his head. He kept sighing and patting my shoulder. "It's all going to be fine, Jenny, my love. You, me and Mommy. Not to worry about a thing."

On the way home, Dad stopped and got us ice cream cones at the Fountain Spray shop. I remember that moment so clearly, the three of us together in the van, licking our double scoops.

Blinkers

Christmas morning and the snowy streets of St. John's were almost empty. Frank was driving across town on a "mission of mercy," as Marie had put it. He turned into the tree-lined driveway of Mount Carmel Orphanage, peering at the imposing building that loomed before him.

Dear God, what are we getting into? he wondered.

"I have an idea, sweetheart," Marie had said one morning in early December. "We should invite a boy from Mt. Carmel to the house for Christmas day. Geraldine Finn and the others in the Catholic League have been doing that for the past few years. It's about time we did our bit."

Frank looked at her from behind the newspaper. "I don't know, Marie. I don't feel comfortable with the idea of inviting an orphan to the house. The poor child might feel awkward in someone else's home, and he'd only have to turn around and go back to the orphanage at the end of the day. That would be cruel."

"Yes, but he'll go back there with a belly full of food and an armload of gifts." Frank flinched at the determination in Marie's voice. "And besides, Frank, it would be good for the kids to learn to share. That's what Christmas is all about. And Brian could do with some company."

Frank, "a big teddy bear of a father," as Marie often called him (not always flatteringly) had been worried about Brian. Timid and on the frail side, he tended to shy away from the rough and tumble with the boys on the street and in his class at school.

Frank sighed, giving into Marie once again. "I guess you're right. It would be nice for Brian to have a friend to play with on Christmas day." He picked up his briefcase and headed for the door. "I s'spose you're always right," he muttered, not without an edge. "What am I going to do with you?"

On a busy Saturday before Christmas, Frank stepped out of his drugstore and walked down Water Street to the Mt. Carmel raffle, an old townie Christmas tradition—buy a ticket on a turkey and help raise funds for the orphanage.

At the door of the raffle, a boy rang a loud school bell, attracting passersby. Inside, Mt. Carmel orphans were selling tickets. "Are they all gone b'ys?" one of the elder boys shouted before spinning the raffle wheel. And the Brothers who ran the orphanage, big brawny men in black robes, stood by, smiling and supervising. The place was crowded with all manner of people, Catholic and Protestant alike, full of festive season laughter. Everyone was feeling good about making a contribution to a worthy cause. Frank even saw one man pressing cash directly into a monk's hands: "You Brothers are a Godsend to this town."

But Frank was apprehensive. Looking at the orphans, he wondered: Is the boy coming to our house for Christmas here today? And who are these children, anyway? What's their life like? He'd once heard a Brother at a Mt. Carmel fundraiser say that homeless children suffer from "the disease of feeling unwanted." Even when his father had taken him to the raffle as a boy himself, he'd felt ill at ease in the presence of these wards of the state. Did he feel guilty because he lived in a nice home with a family, and they didn't? Whatever it was, he still found it disturbing.

"Hello Frank, how are ya?" It was Gus Malone, Grand Knight of the local Knights of Columbus. He shook Frank's hand with gusto, then bored into him with his pale blue eyes. "Haven't seen you at K of C events lately."

Frank stiffened. It was true. He'd been lax about attending K of C meetings.

"You know what it's like, Gus," he replied. "Running the drugstore takes up all my time."

The clanging bell in the doorway was jangling Frank's nerves. "In fact, I have to get back to work right now, Gus. I'll wish you a Happy Christmas and be on my way." He turned on his heels and stepped outside, relieved to get away.

One of the orphan boys ran to the doorway and called after him. "*Wait, sir, you just won a turkey.*"

"Oh, that's okay, I don't need it, give it to someone who does."

"But its yours," the boy said, looking disappointed. "You won it. You bought the ticket from me."

Frank looked at the youth, who was clearly proud he'd sold a winning ticket. "In that case," he said, stepping back inside, "I guess I'd better take my prize."

The boy ran to the counter, picked up the heavy turkey and passed it to Frank with a big smile, displaying his crooked teeth. Poor youngster, thought Frank. God knows what his story is. He patted the boy on the shoulder. "Thanks for looking after me and Merry Christmas."

As he carried the turkey back to the drugstore, he let himself believe that maybe they were doing the right thing inviting an orphan for Christmas Day.

It started to snow—fluffy, white-Christmas flakes—as Frank pulled up to the Victorian doorway of the orphanage. The boy who'd been selected to spend the day with the Powers was waiting on the steps. Frank was moved when he saw him, a tiny little creature standing next to a towering man in black robes. That boy's as skinny as a rake, not a lick on him, thought Frank, wiping a tear from his eye. Marie was always teasing him about being so sentimental, but he couldn't help it.

"I'm Brother Brescon and this is Danny Broyle," said the young monk, smiling as he tousled the boy's curly black hair. "Now Dan, say hello to Mr. Power."

The boy spoke up in a surprisingly firm and somewhat rough voice. "Hello sir, Merry Christmas."

"Now, you make yourself at home, Danny," said Frank as he opened the door to the smell of the raffle turkey roasting in the oven. "Kids, we're here, come say hello."

Little Brian and his teenage sister, Noreen, were sitting on the floor by the Christmas tree. Brian was playing with his Christmas gift, a big plastic rifle, and Noreen was inserting a Bee Gees cassette into her new portable player. She gave Danny a quick welcome wave. Then she pressed a button on the machine and "You Should be Dancing" filled the air. Shedding his usual shyness, Brian jumped up and ran to the door to greet the boy.

Marie came out of the kitchen, wiping her hands on her apron. "Turn that music down," she said as she passed Noreen. Then her face lit up with a smile. "Come on in, Danny, Merry Christmas and welcome. Now Brian darling, help our guest find what Santa left him under the tree."

Danny opened his gifts: a View-Master, a book of fairy tales, a puzzle depicting the Vatican, a package of peanut butter sweets and a bright red home-knit cap. He laid the presents in front of him on the carpet and shrugged his tiny shoulders. "T'ank you," he croaked. Marie raised her eyebrows at the roughness of his voice. Seeing Danny's reaction, Brian came to the rescue, thrusting his plastic rifle into the boy's hands. Danny beamed. And the connection between the two six-year-olds was sealed. They played together all morning, hiding and shooting and riding mock horses.

Things did get a little out of hand: Danny kept dipping his fingers into the holy water font on the wall in the front hall—Marie's pride and joy. It contained water blessed by the Pope, brought back by her parents from their trip to Rome. "What's

come over you, Brian?" she said, surprised to see her usually
timid boy joining in the mayhem. His freckly cheeks were rosy
with excitement, and he'd even flung off the Irish tartan bowtie
she had lovingly dressed him up in for Christmas.

At midday, the family and their guest sat around the perfectly
appointed festive table. "You can sit here next to Brian," said
Frank, taking care of Danny. But within minutes after grace
had been said, Danny began nudging elbows and making fork
attacks on Brian's forearm. Marie lost patience and moved him
next to her. "The table's no place for roughhousing," she chided,
unfolding his poinsettia serviette and placing it on his lap.

Amused, Noreen decided to take an interest in the guest.
"What's it like to grow up in an orphanage?" she threw at the
boy, point blank.

Frank jumped in. "Why don't you ask him what sport he
plays?"

Little Dan wedged a piece of turkey into his mouth. "See, I
never grew up in Mt. Carmel," he said, munching away. "They
just put me in there for this winter. I'm not a real orphan—I got
me own mom and dad. The Brother said I might be goin' home
in the summer, if they gets off the booze."

The whole Power family gaped at the confident Danny.

"Nobody likes it there," he added matter-of-factly. "Tommy
ran away the other day. The police were out looking for him all
night—I saw them dragging him home in the morning. He was
bawling in the doorway because he didn't want to go back in."

Marie's eyes widened. "I'm sure some boys like it there," she
said, counterbalancing. As vice-president of the Catholic Women's
League, this was not her vision of the so-called haven for children
that one supporter had even termed "a footstep from heaven."

Danny looked at her with an expression way beyond his years.
"Well, sometimes the Brothers are real nice but then, before you
knows it, they turns nasty." Then he added brazenly: "When they
hits us, it's a real beating. I saw Brother Brescon banging my
friend Ronnie hard as he could, across the back with a board.

I runs off when I sees them Brothers coming. Yesterday, me and Ronnie hid in the furnace room."

"The furnace room! That sounds scary," said Brian, "Is it dark down there?"

"I heard those Brothers are a bunch of weirdos," said Noreen, availing of the opportunity to goad her mother about the Church.

Marie's eyes darkened. She jumped up and started clearing the dinner dishes with a clatter.

Frank went to find Marie in the kitchen. She was standing by the counter, wiping a tear from her eye. "Not much of a Christmas," she said as Frank comforted her. "It's shocking, the talk that boy's getting on with. Could it be true?"

She pulled herself together and went back to the table with the figgy pudding on a platter. She served Danny first. "You're a grand storyteller, my boy," she said, still a bit shaky, "but you should be respectful of the Brothers who look after you so well. We're lucky to have them here in Newfoundland. They're a teaching order with long years of experience dealing with children."

Danny had the good sense to eat his pudding in silence.

After dinner, Brian and Danny spent the afternoon playing in Brian's room. Before teatime, Frank called the boys downstairs. "Time to get Danny's coat and hat now, Brian."

"But Dad, we're having so much fun. Can't Danny stay the night? Why does he have to go back to that scary place?"

"Not tonight, Brian. Maybe Dan can come back some other time." This is what Frank had dreaded—having to extract the boy from the warmth of this home and drive him back to the orphanage. It had been hanging over him all day.

The winter darkness had already set in as Frank and Danny drove down Elizabeth Avenue, past the houses with Christmas lights twinkling on the fresh snow, back to the orphanage. When they got there, they saw the shadowy form of Brother Brescon waiting inside, behind the bevelled glass doorway. Danny jumped out of the car with his armload of gifts. "T'anks for the good time," he said with aplomb.

Frank watched the monk as he opened the door. *I think I recognize that Brother from somewhere. Where have I seen him before?*

Danny darted in through the doorway.

On the way back home, the image of Danny in the scary furnace room flashed through Frank's mind. *What a brave little soul. Plucky little bugger.*

That night, before going to sleep, Frank found the courage to mention Danny to Marie. "That's a pretty bleak picture the boy paints of the orphanage. I'm concerned."

Marie turned her head away on the pillow. "To tell you the *truth, Frank, I'm not sure what to make of it." After a moment,* she turned back with a dose of her old determination. "He must be exaggerating," she said, as if convincing herself. "The boy's a bit on the wild side, and the Brothers have to keep control. But they wouldn't hurt those children. That Danny's blown everything up in his child's mind." She snuggled in. "Don't go making something out of nothing, now, darling." Frank stared at the ceiling. *That's me, promptly put in my place again.*

Brian caught a bad flu at school in January, and it turned into pneumonia, leaving him weak and coughing. "His spirit is down," said Frank to Marie. "And he keeps asking for that Danny Broyle to visit again."

Frank knew by the slope of Marie's shoulders that she didn't want Danny back in the house.

"I don't think that boy is suitable," she said, heading for the kitchen door. "Why don't we invite one of Brian's schoolmates? At least we know what they come from."

Frank ran to the doorway, blocking her way. "Come on now, Marie, Danny's a good enough little fellow. And Brian needs help recovering."

Brian's recovery was the clincher. "Well, you make sure you keep an eye on that ruffian while he's in the house. God only knows what he could get up to."

The next Saturday afternoon, Frank went to Mt. Carmel to pick up Danny. Once again, Brother Brescon was standing on the front step, with his hand on the child's shoulder.

Frank had a sudden flash. Now I remember who that Brother is—he's the new coach for the Holy Cross hockey team, the one they call "Brother Brute," because he's so rough on the boys. Oh well, I guess there's no harm to it. He really has knocked that team into shape—they've been top of the line all season.

As soon as he saw Frank appear in the driveway, Danny slipped out from under the Brother's hand and ran down the steps. The car had barely come to a full stop when the boy opened the door and jumped in.

As they drove off, Brother Brescon gave what seemed to Frank to be an exaggeratedly cheerful wave of the hand. "That was a speedy departure, Danny. Shouldn't you have let the Brother say hello," he said, laughing to dispel the feeling that something was wrong.

Danny gave Frank a defiant look and put his feet up on the dashboard.

"What are you doing? Put your dirty feet down my boy, and sit up straight," said Frank, shaken.

Marie was in a tizzy because the president of the Catholic League was coming over with her husband for a drink that afternoon, rather than the next day as planned. Wanting to make a good impression, Marie would have preferred to have "just the family" in the housebut the guests had asked to change the date at the last minute.

Brian was feeling stronger now, and it wasn't long before the boys started a round of hide and seek in the upstairs bedrooms, slamming doors and shrieking. In the middle of their antics, Phyllis and Bob arrived and were escorted into the living room for their drink of rum. They were a rather stiff, childless couple. Noreen made a brief, petulant appearance. Then, when summoned to say hello, Brian and Danny came running down the stairs in their underwear, all giggles and devilment. As they raced by, Frank was shocked to see a deep purple bruise on Danny's back.

"Blessed Mary! What are you up to?" said Marie, trying to make light of things. With that, Danny pulled Brian's underwear down and went running back up the stairs. Brian stood there, confused, his tender little-boy penis on display.

Frank pulled his shorts up and scooted him out of the room while Marie explained. "We try to be charitable and let that little orphan from Mt. Carmel come visit from time to time. But he's turning out to be too vulgar to have around."

Bob and Phyllis nodded their heads wisely. "You can only imagine what kind of background those boys come from. Rough and tough, I guess," said Bob, popping a cheese ball into his mouth. "I've heard they live the good life in that orphanage, hearty meals and ice cream on Sundays. And yet they say those youngsters complain, don't appreciate anything."

Frank frowned. "Well, it's only right that they receive the basic things any child should have."

Marie intervened nervously. "What Frank means is... those children deserve to be well-treated. And I'm sure you agree. Now, can I refill your glass?"

"I'm concerned about Danny," said Frank, as soon as the guests were out the door. "Did you see the bruise on his back when he came into the living room?"

Irritated and distracted, Marie turned away and started cleaning up after the cocktails. "I'm sure the orphanage is looking after that, Frank. Now hurry up and take that child home. I think we've had enough for one day."

Frank went upstairs to find the boys in front of the TV.

"Come on now, Danny, time to get your coat and cap."

Danny kept his back to Frank, refusing to take his eyes off the screen. Flustered, Frank picked him up by the armpits. "Sorry, my boy, but we have to get going." He rushed Danny down the stairs and out the door.

Marie raced upstairs to comfort Brian, who was wailing and wailing, "Why does Danny have to go back there?"

On the drive to the other side of town, Frank's hands were tight on the driving wheel. "What ever came over you, my boy?" he said, softly. "You can't be acting like that."

Danny pulled his little body into a ball. "I hate you all! I heard those people, what they said about me being rough. My dad says I'm as good as you or anyone else."

There was no one waiting for the boy at the orphanage door. Frank watched from the car as he rang the bell. It took a while before the door opened and "Brother Brute" came out, looking none too pleased and scary, for sure. Danny stepped into the dimly lit porch.

Frank felt a wave of immense sadness come over him. I never should have listened to Marie. I knew it would all end up like this—cruel and hard. Too cruel for words.

***

Years later, the awful things Frank had imagined about the orphanage finally materialized into a full-blown national scandal.

"Surely, it's only a few Brothers who've been overworked, short-staffed, lonely," said Marie, putting the newspaper down.

"Lonely!" said Frank with a force and conviction that made Marie raise her eyebrows. "Those men are being *criminally charged* for abusing children. It's been going on for years and would still be happening if that janitor hadn't stepped up and reported to the police that he was finding petrified little boys hiding in the furnace room."

He leaned across the table and touched Marie's hand. "Remember the bruises we saw on Danny Broyle's back?"

At the mention of Danny, Marie withdrew her hand.

"It's no sense trying to deny it, Marie." Frank picked up the newspaper. "See, one of the men being charged is that burley Brother Brescon, who 'looked after' Danny."

Frank mustered his resolve. "You're not going to like this, but I got Noreen to help me find out where Danny and his parents are living—government social workers can consult child welfare records and she snuck a look at Danny's file. It turns out he's been in trouble with the law and is on probation for theft and drugs. And it broke my heart to hear this, but he was at Mt. Carmel until he was twelve. He's the same age as Brian. So he'd be 19 now. God only knows what he's been through." Frank's eyes glistened.

"So I've made a decision—we have to let his folks know what we saw all those years ago. Maybe they need our evidence to press charges."

Marie placed her hands on the table. "If the police are involved, they'll see that justice is served. Besides, Frank, I'm concerned about your blood pressure. You should avoid all this turmoil."

She lowered her eyes. "And anyway, I can't be seen making trouble. You know very well that Father O'Brien has asked me to chair the Pastoral Council committee."

Frank listened as she mouthed the Church's official position, the need for "prayer, forgiveness and conversation" to "reassure the parishioners, calm people down" and not "stir things up."

He shook his head. "Marie, the world is moving on. You don't have to keep supporting the Church. Times are changing. Sure, the Berlin wall just came down! Can't you see you're protecting the wrong people? It's those boys and their families who need support. I know you care about those little orphans as much as I do."

"Of course, I feel for those poor youngsters. But is there any need for our family to get involved? It's really just a matter of a few bad apples. Isolated incidents."

Frank called and made arrangements to meet Danny and his parents, but Marie remained steadfast about keeping her distance.

On a blustery March afternoon, he walked up Barter's Hill to the Broyle's basement apartment. I'm finally doing the right thing, he thought to himself as he knocked on the door.

A thin man with sharp features and a front tooth missing answered. "I'm Tim Broyle, Danny's father," he said, with the same direct confidence Frank had seen in the little boy all those years before.

Frank stepped into the low-ceilinged front room, where a petite woman in faded jeans was sitting on a sagging couch. "I'm Danny's mother," she said, nervously tapping her leg with her fingers. "He's gone to a meeting with his probation officer, but he'll be home soon."

"Tell me," said Frank, grasping his hat, "How's Danny doing? Did he get to finish school? He's smart, that boy of yours."

"Oh, Dan's had his problems," said the mother, getting right to the point. "He's been all tore up since Mt. Carmel."

Frank's blood pressure spiked.

The mother tapped her fingers harder on her leg. "He wasn't supposed to stay in that hell hole so long. We tried to get him out, but they kept telling us we couldn't have him. We weren't drinkin' that bad, he could have come home. Bloody monsters. No one cared."

Tim Broyle gave Frank a hard look. "So what was it you wanted to talk to us about?"

Frank lowered himself onto the edge of an armchair. Sweaty and fumbling, he undid the buttons on his overcoat and started in. "With the police investigating Mt. Carmel, I thought I should tell you that when Danny came to visit us, in 1976, my wife and I saw a bruise on his back." He paused, dropped his head. "And he did tell us that he was afraid of being beaten, and he was hiding from the Brothers in the furnace room."

Tim Broyle lit a cigarette and sucked on it. "And you're only giving us that information now? Dan told us years ago about what those Brothers did to him. Other boys are pressing charges, telling their stories on TV. But Dan can't face the police. Gets the shakes if you mention it. He just can't be talking about it. The social worker said he'd try to get him in to see a psychologist, but that could take ages. For now, the doctor's after putting him on tranquilizers."

The mother stopped tapping her fingers. "What I don't get is: If you knew he was being beaten, why didn't you do something? You must be in with all those big wigs." She raised her voice. "What the hell were you waiting for?"

Frank responded, choking on his words. "Believe me. I'm ashamed of myself. I suspected he was being badly treated, but I took that little boy of yours back to that orphanage." Tears came to Frank's eyes. He could barely stop himself from sobbing. Mr. and Mrs. Broyle gaped at him.

Danny's father stubbed out his cigarette. "Lots of people in town knew what was going on. But those boys are lower class, see, so they didn't count, a lower breed. They didn't count."

"You're right," said Frank, agonized. "Those children were... invisible, to me and to everybody. It's like we were all wearing some kind of blinkers." Then he stopped and there was silence as he looked at the Broyles—their tired, knowing eyes.

"I'll do anything I can to help Danny, anything," he said, running his hands through his hair.

"A lot of good that will do now," said Danny's mother. She stood up, looked towards the door. "Anyway, looks like Danny's been held up somewhere."

Frank put his hat on. "Oh, yes... maybe I should get a move on."

He scurried out the door and faced into the wind on Barter's Hill. As he was rounding the corner onto Casey Street, he saw a thin young man with black curly hair coming towards him. It had to be Danny. As the boy approached, Frank reached out his hand. "Danny, I'm Frank Power. Do you remember coming to visit at my house when you were a youngster?"

Danny looked at Frank with dull, empty eyes. No sign of the lively little boy who'd played with Brian. "Yes, I remembers," he said, deadpan, in his recognizable rough voice.

Frank patted Danny's shoulder. "You've grown up to be a big man." He looked into the youth's sallow face, the cuts and bruises on his cheeks, like he'd been in a fight. "I'm glad to see you again, Dan. My son Brian still remembers you. He's at the university now. Hopes to go into law."

Danny gave Frank a look of utter disdain.

Frank added impulsively, "Maybe you could come over to the house. You're welcome anytime. Brian would love to see you." He reached inside his coat and took out a business card. "Here's my phone number."

Danny didn't take the card. As he stood there in his worn parka, anger rose in his eyes. "What would I want to go to your house for? You're just like all the rest of them. You could care less about the likes of me. You can fuck off. Just fuck off!"

He turned the corner, pulling his hood up against the sleety wind.

Frank stumbled off through the skuds of March snow.

On Strike!

"We're working as fast as we can, sir," says Jack, struggling to keep a civil tongue. "But there are rumblings of a longshoremen's strike and that may hold things up."

The inspector gives Jack one of his condescending looks. "Yes, but look here, Warren, as manager, you should be anticipating problems. British Overseas Shipping does not leave cargo sitting around on the wharf."

Jack clenches his jaw. "Of course, sir. As I say, we're doing our best to meet the shipping date."

He heads out to the dock, shaking his head. Why did this idiot have to turn up from England now? An annual inspection just when a strike's looming. What else can go wrong?

This year, the home office has sent out an inspector with precious little shipping expertise. Some company director's snooty nephew, called Barnaby Wakes. He's been hanging around the harbourfront office for the past two weeks, wearing a pretentious cravat and lording it over everyone. Barnaby Wakes. What kind of name is that?

And oh my God! Jack is sweating to get everything in place before Wakes finishes his report. The premises needs work. Some of the timbers on the dock are rotting. And the books are in a mess, a gigantic mess. Shipping notices entered incorrectly, cargo recorded as going off in the wrong direction on the wrong date.

The shipping records are down to the new clerk, a sallow youth by the name of Earstwhile Pitt. Where do these names come from? Jack hired him in a rush and out of pity—an outport boy with some education but no prospects, seeking his fortune in town. But it seems polite young Earstwhile is partial to the drink. Even hides a flask in his desk drawer. This morning, his eyes were glazed over by the time the noon day gun went off. No wonder there's ink blots all over the logbook!

Jack does his best to keep things ticking over in an orderly manner, but he's not entirely suited to the cut and thrust of the shipping world. The real Jack comes to the fore in his workshop, tucked away in the basement of the family house on Larch Crescent, where he patiently, lovingly builds models of Tudor warships, galleons and caravels. This is Jack at his happiest: filing, sanding, and gluing together the many tiny parts of those able vessels that once crossed the Atlantic and sailed right into St. John's harbour. Admittedly, he doesn't always achieve perfection with his assembling. Sometimes he completes a model only to find he has left out a key piece: a binnacle, a bollard, a hull plank or a mast cap. But no matter how imperfect the end result, putting together these replicas gives Jack a satisfaction he rarely gets from his work on the waterfront.

"The dockers are threatening to strike by the end of November," he complains to his wife, Sandra, over his evening rum and coke. "It's been nothing but strike after strike for the last few years! Not that I blame the men, really. They hardly ever get a fair deal. And their prospects are so poor. But I'm worn out with it all. You can't make anything stick in this job—fish cargos are constantly up and down, and if it's not last-minute vessel transfers, it's union demands. As soon as you get things put together, they fall apart on you. A never-ending string of messes to clean up."

"Oh, that's just the way of the world, dear," says Sandra, brushing away the problem in her inimitable fashion. "You shouldn't pressure yourself so much. Lately, you've had a permanent frown on your face."

Sandra Warren is not one to worry about the messes of this world. Other women on Larch Crescent keep their houses neat as a pin—flowerbeds manicured, puffy lace curtains draped nicely in picture windows—but at the Warren's place, weeds run wild, curtains hang askew and the garage door gapes wide open to display "utter chaos," as Mrs. Purcell next door bemoans.

Inside, the kitchen is piled up with art equipment. Sandra Warren is driven by one desire—to get her images on the canvas. Her easel is set up in the breakfast nook, where she spends hours splashing paint. Right now, she's working on a frenetic still life: blood red apples leaping out at you and a fat blue tea pot vibrating with angst.

Her eyes fixed on the canvas, she calls upstairs to her two teenage daughters. Her voice is silky smooth, not at all a reflection of the rampant mind behind it. "Darlene, Faith," she intones. "Come down here. We need to get started on supper."

Darlene thumps down the stairs and comes sulking into the kitchen. Hands on her hips, she confronts her mother. "Why do Faith and I always have to peel the potatoes? The boys don't lift a finger. It's not fair."

Sandra Warren is an unusual mother for the times. She's a bit of an eccentric, you might say. Not that it takes much to be deemed eccentric in 1950s St. John's. "Yes, I see your point, Darlene," she responds. "The lot of a girl is not really fair, and you're right to protest. But the truth of the matter is, your brothers have to be given time to do their homework—they need to get good marks, do well, because, being boys, they'll end up running the world. Look at the brunt your father has to bear at work. That's the lot of a man."

"And we end up bearing the brunt of feeding them and cleaning up their messes," says Faith, who's just come into the kitchen, flicking her strawberry blond ponytail. "Our new dance teacher, Miss Claridge, says women need time to develop their own talents—a bit like you, Mom. Miss Claridge—she says we can call her Penny—even went to New York to take a modern dance course."

Sandra keeps painting, adding a dab of blazing yellow, problematizing a bland banana. "That Miss Claridge seems to have you two all fired up. No harm to it, I guess," she adds, half distracted. "Your father and I want you to achieve, like the boys. But women have a certain role to play, however unfair. That's the way of the world."

"Oh, you always say that, Mom," declares Darlene. "Why can't the world change? Sure, we're almost into the 1960s! Penny says we're entering a whole new era. And women will shine!"

"No doubt, they will," says Sandra, amused. "And, no doubt, you two will do your bit to make that happen!"

Sandra stands up and gives the stove a vague look. "We'd better start scrambling up some supper. Your father'll be coming in that door any minute."

It's been a rough day down on the dock. Jack's late getting home tonight. He comes into the kitchen, takes off his fedora hat and looks around for a place to put it down. The counters are piled high with varying pieces of ephemera, boat model magazines, brushes and paint. He plonks the hat on a chair and the cat promptly jumps up and snuggles into its warm felt fold.

"What a day!" says Jack, frowning again. "If the longshoremen go ahead and strike this week, we'll simply end up failing the inspection."

"Remember what I said about pressuring yourself, darling," says Sandra. "You never know, the strike may be averted."

Byron and Henry—strapping sixteen-year-old twins—come running downstairs. They're going to be late for hockey practice because their mother forgot (once again) to go to the bank, and there's no money in the house to buy bus tickets.

"Alright, in the name of God, I'll give you a ride to the stadium," says poor Jack, who needs to give it up for the day. He turns on a dime and off they go: a tangle of hockey sticks and parkas, with Jack's rumpled hat bobbing behind them out through the door.

"And that's another thing," says Darlene to her mother, who's back at her easel. "Around here, hockey seems to be more important than anything Faith and I are doing. You and Dad know we're interested in dance, but you won't take us seriously."

She twirls, flinging out her arms and knocking a wobbly pile off the counter.

Just last night, the indignant girls lobbied their parents for permission to attend after-school practice sessions at the "Pirouettes" studio on Gower Street. Their father flatly denied their plea, on the grounds that at thirteen and fourteen, they were not old enough to be going home from the studio in the dark November afternoons, especially in that unsavoury neighbourhood. Saturday morning classes would have to suffice.

"It's like your father told you," says Sandra. "We'll support you in whatever you do but don't go pushing the boat out too far. You girls are turning into a real pair of suffragettes. Now, you'd better get on with those potatoes," she mutters, falling deeply back into the whirl of colours on her pallet.

The next morning, just as he's leaving for work, Jack receives a call from the Employers' Negotiating Team, informing him that there is now a real likelihood of a strike involving all the longshoremen in the port.

When he gets to the dock, a gang of angry labourers is waiting for him at the door of the shipping office. Jack usually gets along with the dockmen and has always tried to be as fair a manager as possible. Having suffered long years of distain from the colonial masters at the main office in Poole, he's careful not to ruffle his workers by talking down to them. But on this raw November morning, with foreboding clouds hanging over the Narrows and the scent of snow in the air, the men are particularly riled up.

"Good morning to you, Johnny," says Jack evenly to the ringleader, a tough little wrestler, all muscle and bravado in an oversized wool coat.

"No time for your niceties this morning," yells Johnny. He points at Jack with a nicotine-stained finger. "We wants our demands met—job security, no more layoffs. We've got families to feed. We need fair treatment."

Jack gently shoulders his way into the crowd. "Well, the strike hasn't been declared yet, so you fellers go on back to work and let your union negotiators move things along. They're doin' their best for you. Come on now b'ys, get that fish loaded for Montreal."

He makes it inside, only to find equal pandemonium in the office. His secretary, Donna Kelly, a plump and loyal young woman, comes to his desk with the bad news that the company in Montreal wants the cargo to be sent by rail right away, to avoid the risk of having their freight sitting on the wharf for the duration of a strike. "Earstwhile Pitt took the call," said Donna breathlessly, "And he didn't know what to do so he passed the problem off to that Barnaby Wakes. And now he's gone ahead with railway arrangements without consulting you, Mr. Warren."

Jack looks across the office at the tall, spindly Englishmen. That idiot thinks he owns the world. Before confronting Wakes, he runs through the "Tips for Effective Leadership" he learned from that best-seller, *How to Win Friends and Influence People*: "Don't condemn. Encourage. Keep smiling."

"You've been busy this morning, Mr. Wakes," says Jack, grinning away as if he were at a garden party. "But you see, we'll lose a lot of money if we send that cargo by rail. So we're rushing to load the freight onto the ship before any strike happens."

Wakes simply twitches his nose and allows that Jack was late getting in so someone had to step up and make a decision.

Jack gets busy undoing the mayhem caused by the supercilious Wakes. The workers are loading the freight onto the ship, but only at half their normal pace. Jack can hear the intermittent creaking and squeaking of the winch, ancient equipment about to be replaced by modern mechanization that will require fewer labourers to operate.

The men are agitated, singing the old port strikers' song, written in their honour by Johnny Burke, the "Bard of Prescott Street," as he was known. "We are the men today that will strike for higher pay, we are the bone and sinew of this land."

Jack despairs as he watches them from the office window. How are we ever going to stave off a strike? With the new equipment coming in, those dockmen will be faced with nothing but layoffs. They know they're doomed.

Night comes in dark and early, and it begins to snow, the first snowfall of the year. By 5 o'clock, it's coming down thick and hard, so everyone downs tools and goes home. Half the Montreal cargo remains on the dock. Jack turns off the office lights, locks the door and heads out to his car, into the snow-covered world. Now the wind is picking up. Signal Hill and the South Side are lost behind a wall of swirling whiteness. Just what I need, thinks Jack, steeling himself against that quintessential St. John's mess of sloppy wet snow blowing straight into his face.

And then, oh my God! he remembers that last night, under pressure from his two irate daughters, he relented and agreed they could go to the Pirouettes dance studio after school, but only if they waited for him to pick them up. He gets the car out onto Water Street and tries to turn up Prescott—more of a steep mountain than a street. There's the roar of engines and smell of burning tires as cars slip and slide on the impossible hill. Jack turns the car around. No vehicle is getting up Prescott Street this night of our Lord. He parks on the waterfront and goes it on foot.

Back at home, Henry and Byron are shooting pucks in the living room. Since no one ever uses that room, Jack and Sandra caved in a while ago and allowed the boys to push the furniture back to put a goalie net in there. Jack's one condition was that the boys shoot low, so as not to damage his prize Tudor warship, a slightly wonky replica of the *HMS Victory*, displayed on a dusty shelf over the couch.

Prompted by a loud bang, Sandra calls to them from her perch at the easel: "Now be careful and shoot for the net."

But too late—a puck shoots through the picture window. Sandra and the boys rig up a cardboard repair solution and stick it over the hole to keep out the driving snow. "Mrs. Purcell is going to love this," chuckles Sandra.

Eventually the girls arrive, delighted they've made their way home through the storm on their own.

"Dad didn't turn up and buses can't get up the hills," says Faith, shaking the snowflakes from her hair. Sandra raises her eyebrows as the girls recount their adventure, especially when they get to the part about throwing snowballs at boys from the Brow who followed them up Long's Hill.

"They were a bit on the rough side," says Darlene, giggling. "You should hear how they talked. But I don't know why people from up there have such a bad reputation. They seemed really nice."

"Really nice? Don't be telling your father that. Those are the very boys he doesn't want to see you with. Girls your age have to watch yourselves."

Jack trudges in an hour later, his moustache encrusted with snow. He stands in the doorway, beyond weary.

"Did the girls get home safe?" he calls into the kitchen as he takes his boots off.

Faith pops her head around the corner. "We're here, Dad. Got home ages ago. We walked all the way."

"Thank God you're safe. That's the first and last time I'm letting you go to that dance studio after school. From now on you'll go straight home."

Darlene whams an empty pot into the sink. "That's not fair! The boys get to go to hockey practice on their own."

Jack sits at the table. "Don't be tormenting me with your wants tonight. Today's been just one disaster after the other.

A November snowstorm, a meddling inspector from England, a load of salt fish still sitting in barrels on the wharf and a strike hanging over me. Now, enough of those long faces, girls. Stop your surliness and help your mother with supper."

The two girls serve left-over pea soup along with the doughboys they've attempted to make—an act of love but alas, not of culinary artistry. Smirking, Byron points out in his newly-broken, deep voice that the doughboys are like cannonballs, and that the girls should learn to how to make them light and fluffy.

Darlene gives her brother an angry poke. "No, *you* should learn to make them. There's more to life than flicking pucks around."

"I don't see why you get more allowance than we do," adds Faith. "You guys don't do anything but make trouble around here."

Henry explains in a kindly-big-brother way, that he and Byron are older, about to finish Grade 11 and go out into the world, so they need money in their pockets.

"So do we," clips Faith. "Our dance teacher, Penny, says girls have got to learn to be independent."

"That's enough kids. I can't take any more protest today," Jack says. He picks up a fresh copy of his favourite magazine, *Model Ships: Tips and Tricks,* and descends the stairs to the basement.

"It's just not fair," says Darlene as she takes the leftover doughboys to the trash. The soggy dumplings hit the bin like lead.

The next morning, the sky is a rich blue.

Taking a last gulp of tea, Jack says, "Now Sandra, don't forget, the overseer from Poole is coming for dinner tonight. God knows I don't need that on my plate today, but this Wakes fellow has got to be wined and dined. You'll have to get that living room window fixed somehow. Call Harris and Hiscock and see if they'll do it."

Sandra gives her husband an empty smile and an unconvincing nod. "Okay, darling."

Jack shoos the cat off his hat and puts it on. "And girls, please help your mother cook the dinner. But for God's sake, don't be trying anything tricky like doughboys."

Darlene and Faith exchange resentful glances.

"Don't worry, Jack. We'll put a nice meal on the table," assures Sandra, the very queen of dinner parties herself. "We'll be ready for his lordship when he turns up."

Jack gets out of his cab at the waterfront to find the dockworkers milling around in the bright winter sunshine, buzzing with strike talk. "By the end of this day, we'll be out," shouts Johnny Payne, the rabble-rouser.

Jack reminds them that they're not on strike yet and still on the payroll. "So get to it and load the rest of that Montreal freight."

In the office, everyone is ramping up for the work stoppage. The phone is ringing non-stop. Barnaby Wakes is at a loss for what to do but keeps poking his nose in here and there, trying to get in on the act. "What if the freight doesn't get loaded in time? That could be very costly," he says, stating the painfully obvious to Jack, who's on the phone with the Employers' Negotiating Team.

Jack puts his hand over the receiver to answer Wakes. "Yes, yes. We need to hurry the men along," he mutters, preoccupied by news of last-minute deals.

Unbeknownst to Jack, Wakes strides out onto the dock, clears his long skinny throat and orders the men to increase the size of the loads being lifted by the old winch. "Hurry up now, chaps," he exhorts, adjusting his cravat.

The men try to protest. They know the hoisting tackle on the old winch can't handle the extra weight. But Wakes insists he has no time for insubordination. The freight must be loaded by the end of this day.

Johnny Payne cocks his hat, displays a devilish smile, and shouts out: "Come on b'ys, we better do what the big boss man says."

The labourers shrug their shoulders, then go ahead and implement the Englishman's nonsensical order.

It doesn't take long before the winch comes to a halt with a loud clank, and a top-heavy load tips over, sending barrels crashing down and the cargo of salt fish spilling out onto the wharf.

Jack hears the men shouting and rushes outside.

Wakes runs up behind him and taps him on the shoulder. "Look here, Warren," he says, turning up his nose at the sharp smell of salt fish in the air. "Is there no mechanic on site to fix the winch?"

Jack goes to answer him but can't talk. The words won't come out.

The men start picking up the stiff split fish, their feet crunching on the rough salt spilling out of the barrels. And they're still singing at the top of their lungs: "For our rights we do uphold and for our rights we'll strike out bold."

Jack manages to get his voice box operating. "There'll be no fixing that winch today," he croaks over the din of singing dockmen. "We may have to take a loss on the freight left unloaded. A big loss..."

Earstwhile Pitt appears in the doorway, grimacing in the strong sunlight. "They wants you on the phone, sir," he calls out, with a slight slur. "You'd better come quick."

Donna, the secretary, comes running out, batting the tottering young Earstwhile aside. "Mr. Warren, Mr. Warren," she shouts, pulling her sweater around herself. "There's no strike! They came to an agreement."

Jack throws his hands up into the air and shares the good news with his gang of labourers. "It's been settled, b'ys. Your jobs are safe. No layoffs!"

Wakes stands back, his tall slim frame towering over the rabble of workers. "That's well and good," he says to Jack sternly, as if finally, something has happened that meets his standards.

The men rejoice, choosing to ignore, for now, the future of labour cuts in the offing, like a fog bank sitting outside the

Narrows. They're roaring and singing in deep baritone voices, "We got the terms that we did like. And determined all we made a manly stand."

Wobbly from the emotions of the day, Jack drives up Prescott Street, on to his next challenge—the unavoidable dinner with the despicable Wakes.

He gets home and races into the kitchen, victorious. "No strike! Sandra, it's been resolved. No strike!"

He glances into the living room. "Now hurry up, we've got to get that goalie net out of there." He looks again. "I see the window didn't get fixed," he adds existentially. "What an eyesore! Not up to Wakes' standards, I'm sure." He looks at his watch. "Dear God! He'll be here within the hour! I need a good long swig of rum before I face him. What a day! Thank Heavens the strike's averted."

"I'm afraid your troubles are not over yet," says Sandra flatly. She's standing by the counter, where Jack can see an uncooked chicken sitting ominously in the roaster next to a pile of unpeeled potatoes and carrots. His heart sinks. "What's going on?"

"It's the girls. I went out to Stockwood's to pick up a fancy cake for the Englishman and left Darlene and Faith to make a start on dinner. I just came home to find they haven't done one lick of anything. You're not going to believe this Jack—they've locked themselves in their bedroom and won't come out. They've been het up lately about the boys not helping around the house, and this is what it's come to."

Jack runs upstairs and knocks on the girls' door. "What's got into you two?"

There's a moment of silence before Darlene speaks up. Her voice comes through the door, muffled, but deadly serious, no teenage giggling: "We're on strike!"

Jack cringes at the mention of the word *strike*. He loosens his tie. "On strike?" he blunders. "What are you on about, girls?"

"We're on strike until you promise us the same allowance as the boys. And they've got to start helping with housework. Penny showed us a book she got in New York, all about women's rights. It says in there that it's time to put an end to 'gender-related-chore-distribution.'"

Jack is perplexed but fishes around for a quick solution. "Yes, yes, I see your point," he says, foolishly ignoring the fact that his daughters mean business. "But can't we talk about that tomorrow after we get this dinner party over with? Please, come on out now, girls!"

"We know better than that, Dad. Now's the perfect time to bargain," says Faith. "And if you don't give us what we want, we can stay in here for days. We've got food and drink and everything we need."

Jack looks at his watch. "Okay, okay. We'll up your allowance. And we'll make the boys help with the chores."

The girls unlock the door and step outside, having completed the first in a series of uprisings that will characterize the forthcoming decade in the Warren household.

"And one more thing," says Darlene. "Henry and Byron always find excuses not to help out. Or if they do help, they're useless. You have to make sure they really pitch in. Otherwise we'll strike again."

The kitchen phone is ringing and ringing. Jack races downstairs to answer. It's Wakes, calling to say he caught a chill on the dock and won't be able to make it to dinner. "Ever so sorry to let you down, old chap."

Jack hangs up. "Good news, Sandra. Mr. Delicate English-man's got the sniffles. No Wakes under this roof tonight."

He makes himself a stiff rum and coke. "And my day of strikes is over."

He takes a long swig. "But, you know, I can see nothing but trouble coming up. For sure, those dockmen will be striking again soon."

"Don't despair, Jack," says Sandra, finally committing the chicken to the oven. "At least you managed to settle the girls down."

She calls upstairs, "Darlene, Faith, time to peel the vegetables." She returns to her easel.

The girls come downstairs. "Where are the boys?" asks Faith, in full revolutionary mode.

Jack glances at the window. "They're outside making a hockey rink in the yard."

He opens the kitchen door and calls out, "Byron and Henry, get in here and help with the dinner. We've promised your sisters you'll start doing your part," he adds, casually, as if major changes to "gender-related-chore-distribution" can be made by uttering a few ad hoc words.

The girls are getting on with the job: promptly peeling potatoes and carrots and putting them in the pot, but there's still no sign of the boys.

Darlene confronts her father, firm on her feet, her dark eyes shining. "You're not keeping up your side of the bargain, Dad. The boys are getting away with it again. They should at least set the table."

Jack opens the kitchen door again. "Come on now, boys. You've got to come in and do your bit in the kitchen."

"We can't come in right now, Dad," says Byron gravely. "The ice is just starting to freeze. We have to keep smoothing the bumps out. Otherwise it won't be good to skate on."

"We'll help with dinner tomorrow night," adds Henry weakly.

Jack sips his rum. "Well, you're right about the ice..."

Faith cuts in hard. "There you go putting hockey first again. We warned you about letting the boys get off."

The girls run back upstairs chanting: "On strike! On strike!"

Jack flops down in a chair, frowning again.

"Now don't get too upset about those girls of ours," says Sandra, opening a tube of red paint. "We're bound to have our ups and downs with them. Darlene is strong-willed and look at our little Faith. She's come into her own, a tough negotiator. Times are changing. That's the way of the world."

Like everybody in the family, Jack wishes his wife would not keep repeating that, but he's learned to follow the number one rule for a happy home: Don't try to make your partner over.

He sips his drink. "You know, you're right, Sandra," he concedes. "I may as well go with the times." The worry starts falling from his face. "The girls are going to have their way. And why not? And with the docks being modernized, I'll just have to steer through the labour unrest and do the best I can for the men. Everything will fall into place."

Sandra puts aside her brush and starts to laugh. "On strike! I'm proud of our girls."

Jack smiles. He empties his glass, tucks a well-thumbed copy of *Gluing Techniques for Hull Planking* under his arm, and heads for the basement.

Sandra calls after him in her melodious voice. "Mind you don't glue your fingers together again, sweetheart. It was an awful racket getting them unstuck the last time."

Jack pauses at the top of the stairs. "I think I've figured out how to avoid that now. Mind you, the other day, I did glue my thumb to a plank. With model ships, it's trial and error. But eventually, with patience, you can make it all stick together."

He smiles. "That's the beauty of it."

Goodness

It's 3 a.m. and dead quiet on the ward. Just a few patients moaning, turning over in bed.

Florence is making her rounds. She checks Mrs. Dunne's pulse. Barely a flutter. In a panic, she runs to the nursing office, gets the overnight "on call" list and dials Dr. Hallett's house. The phone rings and rings. Finally, the haughty voice of the doctor's wife answers. "Hallett residence."

"Oh, hello, it's Nurse Patton from the Infirmary. Sorry to call in the middle of the night but Dr. Hallett's patient, Raylene Dunne, has taken a very bad turn for the worst."

"Are you sure she's dying?"

Florence struggles to stay polite. "Yes, I've checked the patient's vital signs. Dr. Hallett did say to call him if she started to deteriorate."

"Well, the last time you woke us up at this ungodly hour, my husband raced off to the hospital and it turned out to be a fool's errand."

Florence sits on her temper. "Mrs. Dunne is in her final moments. I do need the doctor to sign the medical form and bring in the priest for the last rites."

Within the hour, Dr. Hallett comes rushing into the office.

"Sorry about the late hour, doctor."

He smiles, comes a little too close for comfort, touches her elbow and jokes, "When duty calls, you have to answer."

"We'd better get to Mrs. Dunne, then," says Florence, flustered. This is not the first time he's moved in so close.

She follows him down the ward. Was he flirting with her? Hard to say. Maybe he was just being friendly.

Florence pulls the sheet over the dead woman's face. "I really admired her."

"Yes indeed, Raylene Dunne was the finest kind. Thanks for calling me in. I'm glad I got here in time to say my last goodbye. We worked together on the Hospital Foundation, you know, and became good friends. Raylene was a rare bird—a wealthy woman with a sense of giving and a big heart. Too bad she had to go so soon. We were planning to honour her next year: 1963 would have been her 80th birthday."

Back in the nursing office, the doctor is signing the forms. The bright ceiling light is flickering. He looks across at Florence. "Must be hard on you, sitting in here all night in this awful light."

"It does get a little tiresome after a few hours," she admits, still not sure what to make of Dr. Hallett's familiar way. Maybe he's just a kind man, with his soft gray eyes and five o'clock shadow, she thinks. But I wish he'd keep his distance. What if anyone saw us! It's alright for him but I could get in real trouble.

It's 8 a.m. and Florence is finally off work. She walks home, taking the shortcut through Victoria Park. Last night, on her way to the midnight shift, she'd had to veer off the path to avoid a group of ruffians who were drinking and catcalling. This morning it's all sunshine, the only sign of them the broken beer bottles by the bench. Yawning and weary, she pushes on to get home before her daughters leave for school, so she can make sure little Laurie's hair is brushed and Sylvia has her homework done.

"Thank God our girls have you," Evan had said in his guilt-laden letter from prison. "You've got the high spirits and the strength to keep them going. Now all I can hope is that you'll mind that temper of yours and forgive me."

I'll never take him back, not a chance in Hell, thinks Florence, revisiting Evan's letter as she rushes along. He's nothing but a scoundrel. Embezzlement, of all things. How foolish of me to have trusted him. I was swept away by prince charming.

"That won't ever happen again," she says out loud into the morning air.

"Mom," says Sylvia as Florence comes in the door, "the button came off my jacket. It's getting too tight on me and I hate it. I can't go to the teens' roller-skating party at the Stadium in this old thing."

Laurie jumps up from the kitchen table. "Sylvia made me eat porridge for breakfast. She's so mean!"

Florence puts her arms around Laurie. "Settle down now, girls. We'll figure it all out."

She sees the girls out the door, watches them trundle off with their bookbags, down the road to the bus stop. They both need new coats, she thinks. September, and the cold is already setting in, but they'll have to make do for now, poor things. Her mind goes to what her sister Edith said the other day, a proper tirade. "You'll never manage on a nurse's salary. It's a pittance. And that basement apartment is not fit. Cramped and dark, and half the time the phone doesn't even work. It's time to give up on the heroics, Flo. You and the girls should just go ahead and move in with Mom and Dad."

Florence starts clearing the breakfast table. Edith's right about the money, I guess. Two months working at the Infirmary and I'm still barely scraping by. I'll have to find a way. But how?

With the dishes done, she closes the bedroom curtains and tries to sleep. One more nightshift and then back to dayshifts, thank God. As she puts her head on the pillow, Dr. Hallett's cheery smile drifts into her mind.

She wakes up at 4 p.m., to the sound of the girls flying in through the door.

"Mommy, I got a prize for best writing book in Grade 4!" shouts Laurie with glee.

Florence jumps out of bed. "Lucky me!" she calls out. "I'm the goose that laid the golden egg! How did I ever produce such smart daughters?"

Supper over and the girls settled away for the night, Florence finishes pressing their school blouses then heads out to her nightshift. She runs under the stars through the park, almost late for the 12 a.m. start. It's a windy night. She puts her head down and keeps going. I'm always face into the wind, pushing against something, but never mind, I can manage.

She races through the big wooden doors of the Infirmary, into the long hallway with the polished floor and sharp smell of disinfectant. The clock is chiming out midnight. Barnes, the head nurse is just going off duty. "You're cutting it thin, Patton," she says, in that brittle, lethal voice of hers.

"Sorry about that. I was getting the girls' things ready for school."

Barnes buttons her raglan over her portly chest. "Just remember that shifts begin precisely on time. You are responsible and in charge of your ward the minute the hour begins."

Florence looks at her boss's merciless face, over-powdered, with blazing red lipstick on the slit of her thin lips. "I apologize for my lateness. Message received. In the future, I'll be sure to arrive in good time."

Florence goes to the office and sits under the abominable flickering light, frustrated at being caught out. A stomach cramp makes her wince. Oh no, not that again! I've got to calm down. And I better watch it with that head nurse. She hasn't got an ounce of pity for me.

Only recently, one of the other nurses had warned her. "You mind yourself with that Barnes. She's heartless, a jealous witch.

45

They say she's had it hard, lives with her disabled sister and never found much happiness. A slim young Jackie Kennedy double like you would be just the thing to get her fault-finding self going." The nurse had dropped her voice then leaned closer to Florence. "She's friends with Dr. Hallett's wife, you know. Everybody knows that Doc's got a wandering eye, and I've watched him hankering after you—for God's sake, don't ever let Barnes see that."

Florence checks the patients' charts, taking care to prepare the medications precisely. *That's all I need—to make a mistake and get fired.* Then she runs to answer the call-light from the new patient in Mrs. Dunne's old bed. She pushes the door open and enters the familiar room. *I'm really going to miss her,* she thinks.

***

"I'm so grateful for your good nursing, Florence," Raylene Dunne had said one morning a few months before she died. "You're a lovely comfort to me, with your smile and cheerful words."

Florence puffed the pillows and smoothed the blankets. "I'd say you're the one with the good cheer, Mrs. Dunne."

"Oh, you must call me Raylene. No need for us to stand on ceremony. After all, we're both Cape Islanders."

"Okay, *Raylene* it is. I really appreciate your kindness, sending candies to my girls and listening to me go on about my travails."

Raylene grasped Florence's wrist with her spindly fingers. "I know you've had your letdowns. There's bound to be bumps on the road, but we've got to keep going."

"Well, my husband turned out to be a rogue, so I have no choice."

"But you mustn't despair. You may well find your knight in shining armour yet. There's goodness out there, you know."

Florence took her determined stance, hands on hips. "It's hard to believe that, after what happened to me. Anyway, I don't need to be rescued. Especially by some man who'll probably let me down in the end. From now on, I'm on my own. You've got to play the hand of cards life dealt you."

"I see the strong will of the island women in you, Florence. But even they let their guard down and had a good cry every now and then." Raylene's eyes shone as her mind returned to the hills and coves of her childhood. "We Cape Islanders are a rare breed, you know. Coming from those hard times, that beauty and the wonderful goodness of our neighbours."

Through the doorway came the sound of Barnes, berating a young orderly in the hall. "Not good enough at all," she roared.

Raylene lowered her voice, "It can't be easy working under that head nurse. She's not exactly a fount of human kindness. You'd better hop on to your rounds, now, before you get in trouble."

"You're looking ground down, my dear," Edith had said when Florence and the girls were over to her sister's for the regular Sunday dinner.

"Oh, I'm not too bad," said Florence, moving Laurie's water glass away from the edge of the table. She was always mindful the girls might break a piece of Edith's china. "By the way, did you know we have a patient on the ward from the island? Raylene Dunne, widow of that supreme court judge who died last year. She and I have become sort of friends."

"Well, la di da! She's a bit upper crust for you, isn't she? And anyway, I thought they didn't allow friendships with patients on the ward. I heard she's paralysed, bedridden."

"Yes, she had a massive stroke a few months ago, but her mind's as sharp as a tack and there's nothing 'la di da' about her. Raylene came to town, went school-teaching and ended up marrying into the upper class. Then she devoted her whole life to charity work. She's genuine, somehow managed to keep all the goodness of the island in her."

"Oh, there you go again, romanticizing about the island. You've been away for so long, you've turned it into a paradise.

Typical resettlement mentality. It's been almost ten years since we left, Flo. You've forgotten there were as many devils as angels out there."

"That's not how I remember it. People had a bond, a trust, an unspoken pledge to help each other out. A goodness you don't see anymore."

"Well, you're a grand one to talk! She who won't take any help from anybody! You can't battle your way through alone, Flo. Even Joan of Arc accepted help when she needed it!"

Up early for the eight o'clock shift, Florence flicked on the kitchen light and caught Sylvia taking cash from the tea caddy where she kept the household money.

"What are you doing, my child?"

A cluster of two-dollar bills slipped onto the floor from Sylvia's hands. She looked at her mother defiantly. "I need money for a mohair sweater."

Florence burst into anger. "But you know very well we can't afford new things right now. And how dare you try to steal like that. I'm disgusted with you!"

Sylvia flew into teenage drama. "You won't let me have anything anymore. If you can't afford to rear us, why don't you take us home to Nanny and Pop's! I was just taking a few extra dollars to add to my birthday money. I *have* to get a mohair sweater. All the girls are wearing them."

"Never mind *all the girls*," snapped Florence. "You can't be taking what doesn't belong to you just to have your own way. Now put that money back."

On the way to work, Florence's mind was racing. Sylvia was really getting out of hand. Evan always used to say she was her father's daughter—determined to get what she wants, no matter what. Now look what she'd been driven to.

Florence swallowed hard as she started her shift. It wasn't easy to buck up this time.

The sun poured into Raylene's room. She was lying in bed, listening to the news. "They've decided to postpone raising nurses' salaries until next year," she said, in a thin voice. "The government is always dragging its feet. When I was on the Hospital Board, we tried to advance that file. It's an insult how little they pay. You deserve a good wage."

"That'll be the day," said Florence, frowning as she checked Raylene's blood pressure.

"You don't look yourself this morning, Florence. Everything okay?"

"Oh, the girls are wanting this and that. But I can't always afford to meet their desires."

"I hope you don't mind my asking but can't your family help?"

"Well, it's a long story." Florence glanced at her watch. "After Evan went to jail, Mom and Dad wanted to give me their savings but I wouldn't dream of touching that. They've had it hard enough, resettling in that tiny house in Swift Current. My sister Edith buys the odd thing for the girls and pays for dance lessons, and that's already more than she should."

Raylene stirred in her bed and scowled, pointing her nose at the doorway. "Watch out now," she whispered.

Florence turned to see Barnes, standing there, crisp in her starched nursing cap.

"Patton, can I see you for a moment," she said soberly.

Florence scrambled to put the medicine vials back on the nursing trolley and pushed it out the door, passing Dr. Hallett, who was just arriving.

"Good morning, all," he sang out as he headed to Mrs. Dunne's bed.

Outside, Barnes wasted no time, spitting her words out. "Do I really need to tell you you're not being paid to socialize with the patients? And particularly not to be pouring your heart out to them about your personal finances. Know this—I won't tolerate this type of behaviour from you anymore. Mrs. Dunne has enough troubles of her own, especially with her condition worsening."

"Of course," said Florence, flushing and embarrassed, as busy staff and patients flooded around her in corridor.

"On your way home?" asked Dr. Hallett as Florence was going off duty at four o'clock that afternoon. "It's pouring out of the heavens out there. Let me give you a ride." Caught off guard, Florence couldn't find the words to refuse.

In the car, she felt ragged. The day's events had taken their toll. Clutching her purse, she sat as near the door as possible, in the wide front seat of the Lincoln. She peered out the window. What if Barnes saw her leaving in a car with her friend's husband? You hear stories about these doctors. God knows what he's up to with his "wandering eye." And how embarrassing. She didn't want him to see that she lived in a basement apartment on Eric Street.

As they pulled off the Infirmary grounds, the doctor was chatting away, small talk about the construction of the new entrance gate, "a make work project, going on forever." He took out his cigarettes, offered her one. She declined. He's so offhand, she thought. Acting as if a married doctor giving a married nurse a ride home is an everyday occurrence. And he's got that townie talkativeness. At least I don't have to say anything. She glanced around the car—the plush beige leather seats, the Saint Christopher on the dashboard, the doctor at the driving wheel, with his nicely manicured hands, his blue twill sport jacket. In broad daylight outside the ward, he looked older. She could see the wrinkles on his neck, gray hair at his temples.

"It's all corrupt, you know," he said, sharing with her as if they were friends, "those government construction projects. Smallwood supporters getting their payback."

Florence finally piped up. "Thanks for the lift. Such dreadful rain and I forgot to bring my umbrella this morning."

They were turning onto Water Street. "Speaking of this morning, I heard Barnes chewing you out in the hallway when I was in with Mrs. Dunne," he said, point blank.

Florence twitched then focussed on the Saint Christopher.

The doctor kept talking. "You know, in my opinion, that was unprofessional of her. She could have at least met with you in the privacy of the office. Barnes is playing the real sergeant major."

"Well, I probably stayed too long with Mrs. Dunne. The ward was really busy today."

He gave Florence a soft look. "No, honestly, Barnes came down too hard on you." Florence noticed that funny little tic of his—raising his eyebrows and wrinkling his forehead when he spoke. "We all know that head nurses have to run a tight ship," he continued. "There's no room for mistakes in a hospital. But really, you've got to have a heart, too. Mrs. Dunne is going *downhill fast and you're giving her good nursing. I know for a fact she loves your company.*"

Florence nodded her head, not sure how to respond to the kindness coming her way. But he did seem sincere. What to make of it? After all, he's a senior doctor and a married man. With a formidable wife.

It was a short drive and Florence was relieved when they got to Eric Street. "Well, thank you very much, Dr. Hallett."

He grabbed an umbrella and jumped out gallantly to open the door for her. "Take care now," he said, patting her on the shoulder. Florence thought she saw a hint of longing in his eyes.

She scooted away.

Laurie and Sylvia were watching from the doorway.

"Who's that?" said Sylvia, as the car pulled away. "He looks rich. What a car! It's gigantic!"

"Never you mind now, darling. The doctor on duty gave me a ride home because of the rain."

"But Mom, I saw him put his hand on your shoulder. I think he likes you. What would Dad do if he knew this?"

"Don't be foolish. The doctor was just being nice."

"Mommy's got a boyfriend," chanted Laurie. "Mommy's got a boyfriend."

"Stop your nonsense, girls. That's the last thing your mommy's ever going to have. Now, let's get the supper going."

As Florence peeled the potatoes, she thought of a story she'd been told about a former nurse at the Infirmary. The young woman had been swept away by a rich doctor—a fairy tale turn of events. The doctor had left his wife and married the almost penniless nurse. She was now a lady of leisure, ensconced in a sprawling split-level on Elizabeth Avenue and off on trips to Florida in the winter. If I had a rich boyfriend to help me out, thought Florence, it would make life so easy for the girls. For a brief second, she imagined herself pulling down the sheets to get into bed with Dr. Hallett. She shuddered. Dear God, no.

***

It's a crisp October day for Raylene Dunne's funeral. The Basilica is packed. Florence is moved by the priest's homily, praising Mrs. Dunne's belief in community and sharing. On the way out the door, she runs into several people from Cape Island. The warmth of their greeting only heightens the emotion.

Going down the steps, she feels a touch on her elbow and hears a man's voice beside her. It's Dr. Hallett. "They certainly gave her a good send off, don't you think?"

"Yes, it was very fitting," says Florence, keeping her distance.

He turns to his wife, who's firmly linked into his arm. "This is Nurse Patton, from the Infirmary. She and Raylene were the best of friends."

A former beauty queen, Mrs. Hallett is a good-looking blonde, tall and elegant in an expensive camel hair coat, but the effect is ruined by her heavily powdered face.

"Oh yes… Nurse Patton, I think we've spoken on the phone," says the familiar haughty voice. She stops to brush a hair off her husband's coat lapel, tugs his arm in a proprietary manner, then continues. "I believe you work with my friend and bridge partner Edna Barnes. We were in nursing school together, you know. Edna's an outstanding head nurse. I hear she's taking her retirement in the new year. Well earned, I'd say!"

Florence keeps deadpan while experiencing a jubilant inward smile at the news of Barnes' retirement. You might know Mrs. Hallett and Barnes would be friends! They're of an ilk—over-powdered and over-bearing.

Dr. Hallett catches Florence's eye. "Can we give you a ride home?"

Mrs. Hallett knits her eyebrows and clings even closer to her husband.

Florence gives a gracious smile. "Thanks, but no. I'm going to take a stroll to gather my thoughts."

As she starts down the Garrison Hill steps, she thinks: poor Mrs. Hallett's got to do a lot of tugging to keep that husband of hers close to home. A wry smile comes to her face. And Raylene would get a kick of out that: those two witches playing bridge together.

"Flo, I saw in the paper this morning that your friend Raylene Dunne bequeathed a huge amount of money to the Hospital Foundation," says Edith over supper.

"I'm not surprised. Raylene had no children and she was all heart. I must say, I've been missing her these few months since she passed. She used to cheer me up."

"I don't know how much longer you can keep up the grind, Flo. You're nothing but skin and bones and determination. Really, you should consider Mom and Dad's offer."

Florence takes a sip from the crystal sherry glass. "Thanks for your concern, but we're fine for now. The girls know Christmas will be modest this year. I'm just hoping the government will come through with that salary raise eventually. Anyway, I've started doing a correspondence course in nursing administration on my days off, so I can qualify to become head nurse. I think I'd like that, and the pay raise would make all the difference."

Florence plods home through the snow from work, gets into the apartment, takes off her boots and hangs her coat up. Five o'clock and dark out already. She'll be glad when the light starts coming back in the new year.

Sylvia runs to the doorway. "Mom, a big brown envelope came for you in the mail. It looks official. From a lawyer's office."

Florence reads the cover letter explaining the documents in the thick envelope. "Dear God, how good was that woman!"

"What is it, Mommy?"

"Raylene Dunne has bequeathed us some money."

The girls start jumping up and down. "Can we have Christmas now?" asks little Laurie.

"Yes, my darling. Thanks to Mrs. Dunne, we can have Christmas and pay the bills."

Barnes comes into the office as Florence is about to go off duty the next afternoon. "Before you go, I need to talk to you about a serious matter." She closes the door, a glint in her eye—a victorious glint. "You made a big mistake, talking to your sister on the office phone this morning."

"Oh sorry, my home phone wasn't working, and I had urgent news."

"Yes, urgent, for sure. I overheard what you said about receiving a tidy sum from Raylene Dunne. I spoke to you before about fraternizing with the patients. You were forewarned. I've had no choice but report you this time. There's a very good chance you'll have to go before the Board regarding a breach of professional conduct. This could be seen as extortion of money from a vulnerable patient."

Florence's voice comes out shrill. "But that's ridiculous. I was totally surprised by this bequest. I haven't done anything wrong."

"It's no sense yelling at me. The Board will decide the rights of it," says Barnes, opening the door. "The whole affair could well lead to your dismissal."

Florence sits under the flickering light, wincing from stomach cramps again. This could be the end of me. How stupid

I've been! I should have been careful to keep on the right side of Barnes. If I lose my job, I'll have to give in and take the girls home to Mom and Dad.

A few weeks later, with no news from the Board and wracked with worry, Florence starts a new round of nightshifts. It's 2 a.m. and an old man in intensive care takes a sudden turn for the worst. She checks the list of doctors on call. Sure enough, it's Dr. Hallett. She holds the phone to her ear, dreading the encounter with the snooty Mrs. But this time the doctor himself answers. "Not to worry," he says, "I'll be right along."

After the patient's death, Florence finds herself once again in the tight little office with the doctor. "You were right to call me," he says, moving in, this time close enough to give her a whiff of cigarette smoke on his jacket. "Old Mr. Thomas was never going to last the night." He pauses. "And anyway, its just as well, because I wanted to speak to you."

Florence stiffens. What's this now? She can't take anything else.

He wrinkles his forehead. "Today I was invited to attend a meeting of the Hospital Board. They discussed the accusation against you submitted by Edna Barnes. I want you to know that I vouched for your true friendship with Raylene, and the Board agreed there was no misconduct. You are free of all accusations." He gives her a warm generous smile.

Florence draws a big breath. "Oh my God! Thank you so much!" Spontaneously, she reaches her hand out to touch his arm, then quickly pulls it back. "Dr. Hallett, I'm eternally grateful. Now I can keep my job."

"Glad to have you on board. You're an excellent nurse and a fine young woman."

He stands close for another moment. Florence sees a definite look of longing in his eyes. His hand slips into the curve of her back.

"I was hoping we could meet for a drink sometime."

She moves sharply away, gathers up the charts on the desk and holds them to her chest. "If you'll excuse me, doctor," she says, supressing the tremble of anger in her voice, "I have to get back to the ward, now."

He picks up his coat and gives her one last look. "Well, the offer stands if you're ever so inclined. I'll say good night and wish you all the best."

She waits while his footsteps retreat down the hall and the front door opens and slams shut.

In the dead quiet, the office light makes a loud buzz, does a final flicker and goes out. In the blessed darkness, Florence flops into the chair and lets the tears of relief come flooding. I guess Raylene was right, she thinks. Goodness did come my way. A knight in shining armour. Sort of.

Lilacs in the Wind

Purple ribbons. That's what Lydia wore in her hair the day she met Gerry. She'd seen him around town, noticed him and his red-headed good looks. She knew who he was—a trained vocalist, he sang solo sometimes at public events. Gerard Mehan, a good catch, son of a well-to-do Catholic family—but forbidden territory for Methodist Lydia. She travelled different pathways from him, went to a different school and to different church picnics, frequented different households.

But their pathways finally converged on July 12, 1895—a date recorded in Lydia's mind forever—when the Governor came to Grace Harbour on an official visit. Gerard Mehan was the chosen soloist at the welcome ceremony down by the wharf. Everyone in town was there, dressed in their finest— respectful, honoured to be in the presence of Queen Victoria's royal emissary.

Lydia stood in the crowd listening to Gerard's tenor rendition of "The Last Rose of Summer." Drawn by the way he put body and soul into his singing, she filled her eyes with him. As he emoted in the last verse, "Oh, who would inhabit this bleak world alone," a flush came to his face and his Adam's apple bobbed. Lydia shivered, already in love before she'd ever even spoken to the boy.

"You can't be running off on flights of fancy," her mother had said to her just that morning over breakfast.

"But Mom, I want to go live in Boston, like Aunt Tilly."

"Lydia, my child, you know very well that all ended in nothing but disappointment. Life never works out like a romance story. Far from it."

Lydia looked out the sunny window, turning away, as usual, from her mother's hard-knock version of life.

After Gerry's song, Governor O'Brien stepped up to the podium and gave his talk. As he droned on with her Majesty's best wishes to her devoted people, Lydia worked her way through the crowd and placed herself next to Gerry. He was standing in the front, near the spruce arch erected for the occasion.

"I loves your singing," she whispered to him brazenly.

Gerry was surprised, stepped back from the forthright Methodist maid with the peachy cheeks and light blue eyes. But Lydia just moved closer.

And that was the beginning of it. A love match on a summer's day in the sprucy smell of the governor's arch.

Lydia was always drawing pictures. Inky renditions of wildflowers, the cat, her married sister Nora's new baby. But now it was Gerry. His wavy hair, deep-set eyes, the dimple in his chin.

"Meet me tomorrow," she'd said to him at the governor's do. And sure enough, he'd turned up in the shady alcove behind the lilac trees in the Methodist cemetery. Gerry was shy, kept swallowing hard, taking his cap off and putting it back on.

Lydia talked and talked, dreamy, poetic, girl-talk—finally, she had someone to listen to her: "Look at the clouds, they're like big ships leaving the harbour. Can you catch the whiff of lilacs on the wind? They don't last long, here and gone, a moment of perfect happiness!" She swooped her arms like an actress.

Gerry glanced at her askance, afraid of her drama, her boldness.

Lydia touched his arm. Felt the hard muscle under his shirt. "Sing me a song," she said. And he did, as soft and sweet as she could ever have wanted: "A Kiss in the Morning, Early."

And that was the first of a long string of secret meetings and kisses, lots of kisses, in the woods and meadows of Grace Harbour.

A warm summer's morning at their favourite spot, by the lily pond, dangling their toes in the silky water.

"Lydia, my darlin', I've never known a girl like you. So pretty and so smart. Drawing those lovely pictures, a real artist. When you finish school next year you could become a teacher."

"Not me! I want to go away and see the world—the theatres in London, the galleries in Paris."

Gerry shook his head, amazed. "Where did you get all that?"

"I read the stories in the *Lady's Bazaar* magazine my Aunt Tilly sends me from Boston. My mother says my mind's full of fancy. But she's wrong. I'm going to be an artist. As soon as I can, I'm going off to Boston to study art. Don't you want to get away?"

"Not me. I've got to stay here in Grace Harbour and go into the family business," said Gerry, looking responsible, almost manly. "I'm fourth generation Mehan, have to carry on the tradition. This is where I'm planted."

Lydia flinched at the word *planted*—so final, not part of the plans she'd been embroidering in her mind. She'd already imagined herself and Gerry well out of Grace Harbour, married and living in Boston.

All that summer, she coaxed Gerry to meet her, listen to her dreams, be her confidant. They shared secrets, sang together, sketched pictures, walked in the woods, swam in the lily pond. Gerry was charmed. "You're like a fairy, Lydia, enticing me, so lively and pretty and full of wishes."

But despite the enticement, being a Mehan remained central to Gerry's existence. Try as she would, Lydia couldn't change that. "My dad's an important man, he's running for office, you know," he bragged. "John Mehan's going to run this town! And my mom's a force to contend with. I hate to be sneaking behind their backs."

An August evening with the warmth of summer draining from the air. In the shelter of the big cliff face at the entrance to the harbour, the two lovebirds were kissing, their bodies pressing against each other. Lydia was undoing the buttons on her high-necked blouse.

Gerry pulled back, puffing. "My God, Lydia, I shouldn't be touching you like this. You know how sweet I am on you. But it's wrong. I can't marry a Methodist. It can never happen. Sure, my dad's the deacon at Holy Martyr."

"Oh, Gerry, we're like Romeo and Juliet: the Mehans can't mix with the Powells. But we have to be together."

"Do up your blouse, please," said young Gerry with a catch in his throat.

It was around that time that Gerry's older brother Francis, a bachelor and believed to be more than a little eccentric, came back from working in Boston and took a job as a clerk at Pike's Freighting Service. Everybody in town was talking about Francis, who'd been strutting around in a dapper boater hat and spouting new ideas: he'd stopped attending mass to take up something called theosophy, whose promotion of spiritual emancipation he was happy to share with all and sundry.

The devout Mehans were outraged, proclaiming they would not allow a heathen son to live under their roof or take part in the family business. By September, Francis had rented a Spartan set of rooms up over the freighting office. Gerry started dropping by to see him on the way home from school. It didn't take long for Francis to see that something was eating away at his little brother. "What's on your mind these days, Ger? Worried about the future, now that you're finishing school this year?"

Gerry looked pained. "I got this girl on the go, Francis, b'y. She's a Methodist. And it's gettin' serious. You knows Mom and Dad would kill me if they found out."

Francis laughed, slapping Gerry on the shoulder. "So that's what it is! Good for you for stepping out of the family straitjacket!"

Before Gerry left that day, Francis gave him a wink, slipping a key to his bachelor rooms into his brother's coat pocket. "I'm going be working long hours, so you and your young maid can use this place to get in out of the cold."

A windy October day, with leaves blowing off the trees. Gerry and Lydia raced through the door for their first meeting at Francis' chilly rooms. Gerry lit the coal stove. As they warmed their hands, Lydia talked and talked, distressed.

"Oh, Ger, everything's gone wrong! The teacher reported me for talking back to her, just because I said Lord Byron is dull and old-fashioned. Then my mother got mad and said that was the final straw and if there's even a hint of any more trouble, she's going to send me to that strict Methodist College in St. John's." Lydia's tears brimmed up. "I'd be far away from you, Ger. You're the only one who knows and appreciates me."

She threw herself on him. "Take me in your arms. I can't bear the idea of being separated from you."

In the privacy of Francis' rooms, and with Lydia at her most dramatic, Gerry's restraint gave way—on that October day the two lovers lay together in full intimacy.

"Mother of God, I can't help myself," said Gerry. "You're a beautiful temptress."

"Now we're bonded forever," said Lydia afterwards, dewy-eyed.

Gerry looked grave. "It's not all that easy and you know it, Lydia." He jumped off the bed. "Please, for God's sake get up! We could be found out!"

They dressed and went into the other room.

"Sit down," said Gerry. "I have to talk to you." He dropped his head into his hands. "You're too much for me, Lydia. I'm way in over my head with you. It feels unreal, like you're trying to live a fantasy from one of those Boston magazines." His voice was scraping. "And now we're living in sin. What are we going to do?"

"For sure we have to do something, Ger. No one in this town could ever accept a mixed marriage. Who would dare to even perform the ceremony? They're too scared they'll be turned away at the pearly gates. Let's go off to the Boston states, separately, and meet up there. I've got my Aunt Tilly, and your brother Francis must have friends he can send you to."

"It's all too fast, Lydia. You're so sure about everything. And anyway, it's the same thing up there, the divide between Catholics and Protestants. No Mehan can ever marry a Powell. There's nowhere for us to go."

A knock on the door. Gerry put his forefinger to his lips. "Sshhh! Someone's there."

More knocking, then a woman's voice, shrill. "Francis, are you in there?"

Colour drained out of Gerry's face. "It's my mother," he whispered, almost choking.

Mrs. Mehan knocked again. With no response, she rattled the knob of the locked door. Then she went to the window and peered in through the scant curtain.

At the sight of Gerry and Lydia, she shouted: "Well, Blessed Mother of God! Open this door immediately!"

Gerry jumped up obediently, unbolted the lock and opened the squeaky door. His mother loomed huge in her purple coat and hat. "What a disgrace," she said, reverting to a quiet, disgusted voice. "I might have known that Francis would be a bad influence. And you Gerry, nothing but a boy. I've known for a while you were up to something. What's your name now, young maid?"

Lydia fiddled with her blouse button. "I'm Lydia Powell."

"What Powell is that?"

Lydia stood up and gathered herself. "I'm the daughter of Gladys Powell, the postmistress. My father's Gordon Powell. He's a ship's cook." She paused. "Gerry and I want to get married."

"Yes, and I'm the Queen of England!" Mrs. Mehan's buxom chest was heaving. "What ever got into you Gerry? This girl's clearly beneath your station, bold as brass and a Methodist to boot!"

"Lydia's a nice girl, Mom. She's talented and smart."

"Smart enough to go after your money! Can't you see, she'll stop at nothing to get hold of you, pull you away from your family!"

She turned to Lydia and bellowed, "Now then, you get right out that door and don't you dare go near my boy ever again."

Lydia looked at Gerry, but he dropped his head. "Ger, say something," she begged, tearful. But he kept his head down. She picked up her coat and headed for the door, glancing back at him.

And out she went, shaking so hard she could barely make her way down the steep steps to the street.

It was a busy Friday afternoon at the post office that day. Gladys Powell was working behind the wicket when she saw Mrs. Frank Mehan come stomping in. She knew who she was of course, the Mehans being so well-to-do.

What's this, now, she said to herself, as the wealthy matron's big purple hat bobbed its way through the crowd.

Mrs. Mehan reached the top of the line and leaned in over the counter.

"You keep that daughter of yours well away from my boy," she said in whispered rage. "I know about the sin they've been up to." Then she turned and worked her way to the door.

Back at the wicket, Lydia's mother was left with a whiff of expensive violet perfume and the shocking news of what her daughter had seemingly been up to. For a minute, she sat staring into space, her mind and body rigid. Then she heard the voice of the next customer in the lineup, as if far away, saying, "Mrs. Powell, have you had a shock? Are you alright?"

"You're nothing but a shameful waif, not fit to be under this roof," said Mrs. Powell as she served the Sunday dinner. She couldn't stop her moralizing sermons. Her face was contorted with pain. "I'm a woman of standing in this town, Lydia. People need to put their faith in me. What must they think of how you were reared! Cavorting like that, and with a Catholic boy, no less!"

Lydia knew full well the depth of her mother's devastation. After all, she'd deliberately crossed all lines of decency and, as well, all sectarian lines. But her mother's hurt was nothing to the pain she herself was feeling. All she could think of was her Gerry's refusal to stand by her, his dropped head. His total silence.

All fall, she saw nothing of Gerry. Desperate, she kept sending him letters through the mail and despite receiving no answer, persisted, as Mrs. Mehan had predicted.

Determined to eradicate any possibility of the romance re-kindling, Mrs. Mehan called upon Father Cadigan from Holy Martyr church to step in and arrange a meeting with the Powells. At teatime on a Saturday afternoon in late November, the priest knocked on the Powell's door hard. Bang bang bang. Lydia's mother greeted him with a look of defiance. As bad as she thought her Lydia was, she was not allowing all the blame to be on the Methodist side. She led the priest into the parlour.

Lydia's father was home from the boats that week. A mountain of a man with a squint, he sat awkwardly on a straight-backed chair by the window, letting his wife take the lead. Unlike Gladys, he'd shown some sympathy for his daughter. "She just got carried away. It's her artistic temperament."

The clergyman sat down in the plush armchair. Mrs. Powell sat on a chair next to her husband, her shoulders twitching. No Catholic priest had ever darkened the door of the Powell house.

The clergyman looked at the Powells with a benign expression, giving a false little smile, as if he were there to spread good will.

Lydia's mother took in the portly priest with his head full of blond curly hair and his plump cheeks. Those Catholic men of the cloth are well-fed, she thought. They do well by their parishioners.

The priest started right in on business. "I've come to ensure the situation with your daughter gets resolved properly, once and for all," he said in a hushed but firm tone. "She must stop trying to contact Gerard Mehan."

Lydia was behind the door in the kitchen, listening as hard as she could.

Lydia's mother smoothed her skirt with nervous hands. Then she said gravely: "Well, sir, uh, Father, it's more serious than you think. This young man has created an awful situation for himself and for my daughter." She straightened up and held her head as high as she could. "I must tell you that yesterday, I took my Lydia to see the new doctor here in Grace Harbour and he's as much as confirmed that she is with child."

The priest's nostrils flared slightly, but otherwise his expression remained benign. Then, amazingly, he carried on as if Lydia's mother had said nothing at all, blithely ignoring the startling news. "Now I'm sure you'll agree that complete separation is the only road to take. I'm depending on you to go along with this."

Mr. Powell turned his squinty eyes on the priest and piped up: "But what about the state of our daughter?"

The priest stood up. "I'll be on my way now," he said, his robes sweeping past the dumbstruck Powells. "And thank you for your understanding." With that, he went to the door, turned the knob and let himself out.

Lydia stood crying in the kitchen.

"Dear Francis," Lydia wrote, "Please can you tell me where your brother Gerry is? I need to see him. He has to help me."

The note was sent along with Lydia's cousin Perry, who was sworn to secrecy. A scribbled response from Francis was sent directly back. "They've sent him off to relatives in Boston. He won't be back. Sorry for your trouble."

Lydia kept searching for Gerry in the secret meeting places, hoping he would come to find her. How could he go off to Boston without her? But she soon realized that it was true—he'd left her behind in Grace Harbour. No sign of him anywhere. Gone from the hills and the harbour rocks and the meadows. Never to be seen in this place again.

"Now then, Lydia Powell, don't you go out of this house." Her mother's voice was laden with disgust. "No one is to know. Before that bump starts to show, you and I will go to Aunt Ida's in St. John's. And we won't come home until the baby is born. You can stop your bawling and crying. You brought this upon yourself. And you'll have to bear the shame of it."

The baby boy came out looking just like Gerry. Brown hair with a sheen of red, light coppery freckles across his nose.

"Leave it to you to produce a little Irishman," said Lydia's mother in her usual curt manner. But Lydia did see her pick the baby up and even soothe him with a lullaby.

The child was healthy and suckled happily at Lydia's breast. Still an infant, he was brought back to Grace Harbour. The baptism was held promptly, bringing Josiah Powell into the Methodist church. There was no tea held after the christening. The family went straight home and Mrs. Powell laid down the law: "No one must ever know about Josiah's origins. And you mind—you're the boy's older sister, Lydia, and you'll act accordingly."

For appearance's sake, Lydia's mother stayed home with the baby for a brief while, then returned to work at the post office, leaving Lydia to keep house and look after the child.

Lydia spent happy hours nurturing little Josiah. "At least you've lost the urge to get out of Grace Harbour," said her mother. And it was true, Lydia's desire to see the outside world, her brazen will and plans to be an artist, had all dissipated. She still liked to draw every now and then, mostly sketches of Josiah. Everything centred on the boy. A good natured and bright child, he made no fuss, felt equally at home in Lydia's or her mother's arms. But as he grew up, he learned to seek safety behind Lydia's skirts when Mom was scolding.

Mom was stern alright, but she'd firmly taken on her role as parent of Josiah, ensuring that the town could see that he was her son and nobody else's. In church, Joey was duly seated between Mom and Dad, dangling his little legs, while Lydia quietly watched him, smiling and catching his eye, from her place next to her father.

Joey's first day at school. Mom and Lydia took him along, his uniform pressed, his copper curls combed nicely. When they got there, Lydia's older sister Nora was just arriving with her son, Cyril. "Look how grown up my Cyril is!" she boasted. "Already in Grade 5!" Nora was happily married, expecting her third child. Lydia stood back, swallowing her envy as she watched her sister blooming in motherhood. "Cyril's always top of his class," said Nora, gushing. "What a blessing he is! John and I want to keep on having children, a whole tribe of youngsters."

There was excitement in the school: parents and children milling around and chatting. Mom didn't join in the chatter. "Time to go now, Lydia," she said briskly, leaving Joey in the classroom with just a quick pat on the shoulder.

"Wait Mom, let me button his jacket before we leave. He looks untidy."

Mom hesitated, almost bent down to the child, but then turned on her heels. "Don't be mollycoddling the boy."

Lydia sighed, tearing up. What could she do? Mom was always like that with Joey. Standoffish. As if she could only take the pantomime of being his mother so far, as if a slavish sense of decency made her hold back from openly loving this child of sin.

The Methodist garden party in July. Lydia, her mother, father and Joey strolled through the crowd. Lydia was enjoying the summer's day, the lilacs in bloom, the warm breeze. My Joey's growing up fine, she thought, as she watched him play games with the other children. My sweet boy! I feel content. But her happiness was fleeting, like the scent of lilacs on the wind, there and gone.

"Look at that red-headed Powell boy—pure Mehan, by the look of him," said a passer-by in earshot. The woman's nasal voice grated. "They say Lydia Powell went with young Gerry Mehan a few years ago. That old postmistress is not that youngster's mother. His sister had he... his sister had he."

"Come over here right away, Joey," snapped Mom, "and mind yourself with these crowds."

Lydia shuddered. My poor Joey. The town is full of rumours about him. It's so unfair! She gave the boy a loving smile. He smiled back.

He never rocks the boat, always seems happy to be who he is, she thought, despite people gawking at him, and despite Mom's chilly handling.

To Mom's credit, in the privacy of their home, she did have a way of sending tender messages to her ill-born grandson. On Sunday afternoons, she sat at the piano with the boy, teaching him the old Methodist hymns. "Will your anchor hold in the storms of life," she bellowed out. Joey sat next to her on the piano stool, singing along in his lovely tenor voice—Gerry Mehan's son, for sure.

And then there was Dad, big quiet Dad, who was as kind a father as the boy could ever want. "Come to the shed with me now," he'd say, "You're a grand help with the chores."

Lydia knitted and sewed, kept the Powell house clean, stayed home under her parents' roof and took no interest in courting ever again.

"You need to find a husband for yourself," said her mother, as Lydia ironed Joey's school shirt one night. "You can't be mooning over that Mehan fellow all your life. He was an error of judgement. Come on now, do yourself up a bit. You've gone to looking plain."

Lydia pressed the iron carefully into the points of the stiff shirt collar. "This life is enough for me, Mom. I'm happy as I am. Joey's doing well. As long as he thrives, I'm content."

"I wouldn't call you content, Lydia. You used to be high-spirited, God knows I suffered with that. But now you're broken and you're nurturing yourself from Joey. He's growing up now, and will soon be finding his way in the world. You can't live your whole life through the boy, turning his every little joy into your joy, his every little sniffle into your own personal drama. And you mind he never thinks anything but that you're his sister. That's a scandal you'll have to hide for the rest of your life."

But Lydia did wonder if Joey knew that the love in her eyes, in the carefully buttered sandwiches and fluffy blueberry duffs she made for him, was not sisterly but motherly love. Surely goodness he could sense that. Every day of her life, she craved to tell him out loud that she was his mother.

***

Proclamation: Your King and Country Need You! Will You Answer Your Country's Call?

W.E. Davidson, Governor.
The Daily News, St. John's, Newfoundland.
August 22, 1914.

"Sure, all the boys are goin' over, it's my duty."

Joey had grown into a strapping man. He filled the kitchen door frame.

Lydia was at the stove stirring a pot of soup. She turned, her voice cracking, "No little brother of mine's going off to fight in some foreign war to get lost forever."

Mom got up from the kitchen table. "You're only eighteen, my son. Put that right out of your head."

"But Mom, Nora's letting Cyril go over. He and I are signing up together."

"Cyril's twenty-three, that's a different matter."

Josiah steeled his eyes.

He's adamant about doing his duty, thought Lydia. Just like his own father, no swaying him from what he thinks is right.

The letters from overseas arrived months after they were written, dribbling into a household starved for news. Mom let Lydia open them. That's how she handled the situation: little concessions to ensure that Lydia kept control of herself, maintained propriety.

Lydia opened the envelope, gently unsticking the precious paper as if touching the very flesh of the beloved boy. She read out loud, carefully enunciating every word.

> "We had a hard time in Gallipoli, hot as Hades, floods in the trenches and constant enemy fire. But our boys took a ridge and they named it Caribou Hill after the Regiment.
>
> We were four months in Egypt for recuperation and now we've been transferred to France. I've met a French girl in a little town near the front. She's petite with black curly hair, like a Kewpie doll with a bit of the devil in her. I'm already learning a few words of French. Have been to her house, met her family and had a drink of wine."

Mom raised her eyebrows. "Full of his charming self. I know where he gets the courting urge from."

Lydia held the letter to her chest. "Sounds like hell over there, Mom. He needs every bit of loving care he can get." She folded the letter carefully and put it in the buffet drawer with the others, wrapped in a purple ribbon.

There had been no letters from Josiah since that the last one in March. News came through to Grace Harbour that Cousin Cyril was in hospital in England, seriously wounded.

June was almost finished, and Lydia was worried. The newspapers were talking about the British making a big push against the Bosch. "I feel doom in my gut," she kept saying.

Then the horrific news broke. July 1, 1916. The Newfoundland Regiment had been almost wiped out at a place in France called

Beaumont-Hamel. The papers were full of talk of bravery, heroism, sacrifice. Days went by with only scant information on how many were killed or wounded. Mom went to work at the post office, hoping and dreading for news to arrive. Dad spent his time at the window, as if Joey might magically appear on the front steps.

Lydia couldn't eat, couldn't sleep, couldn't be. It was the morning of July 5. She was just bringing a pan of water to the kitchen sink. Glancing out the window, she saw Mom and her sister Nora trotting up the pathway to the front door. Mom was carrying a newspaper under her arm, and Nora had five-year-old Florrie by the hand, the last of her tribe. They came into the kitchen.

Instinctively, Lydia stopped dead in her tracks. Mom unfolded the newspaper with its block letter headline: "Extra. Extensive Casualty Lists. Extra." She pointed to the first list, on the left-hand side of the page.

"The worst has happened, Lydia," she said with all the gravity in the world. "Joey's dead and gone from us all now. Our poor boy never got a chance to be a man."

Lydia looked at the newspaper, saw her son's name: Josiah Powell, believed to be missing in action.

Her hands gripped the rim of the pan.

Mom started sobbing. "Oh, dear God save his soul."

Lydia let go of the pan of water. It dropped with a clang on the slate tiles, reverberating until it finally stopped dead still.

Water crept across the kitchen floor.

Little Florrie wailed.

A shudder started rolling through Lydia, so deeply, it looked like her lithe body would break into pieces.

In a memorial service for Josiah at the Grace Harbour Methodist church, Lydia had to be helped to her seat, she was so pale and wan. Condolences and respects were paid to Mr. and Mrs. Powell, as Josiah's recognized parents, while Lydia sat in the church pew, sobbing. Gerry Mehan's brother Francis attended the service. Being from a Catholic family, he had to sneak in and hide in the shadows at the back of the church, where he quietly mourned the nephew he had seen around town but could never acknowledge.

For a long time, Lydia was tortured by lack of formal confirmation of Josiah's death. After all, he was only *believed* to have perished. Could there be a chance that he would turn up? Then finally, the Colonial Secretary sent written notice that Josiah had officially been declared lost in action. Curiously, the letter was not addressed to Mrs. and Mrs. Powell, but to Lydia Powell (sister). Shivers ran through her as she realized that Josiah had put her name as next of kin (sister) on his recruitment form. Questions raced through her mind. Had he realized she was his mother? Had loose tongues in Grace Harbour dropped hints to him? Had he known all along that his Mehan origins were the not-so-well-kept secret of a small town? If only she had had an openly motherly moment with him before he left! Why had she let social taboo hang over her love for her son! For the rest of her days, she would carry this regret, a wistful sadness on her shoulders.

More documents arrived in the mail, inviting Lydia to negotiate a pension in compensation for Josiah's death. Following the strict military bureaucracy, with each response to the paymaster, Lydia duly signed, "Lydia Powell (sister)."

Lydia settled into the solitary life of a childless spinster, visiting her sister Nora most days, to slake her loneliness. At suppertime, she put on her shawl and headed home to make a meal for her parents. "Poor Lydia," Nora could be heard to say, as she watched her go off. "No life of her own. And old before her time. So unfair, what happened to her."

"Be careful how you go now, Lydia," Nora called out.

"Don't worry, Nora, I'll be alright," Lydia called back, as if resigned to her fate.

Exactly nine years after the slaughter of the Newfoundland boys at Beaumont-Hamel, a large package came in the mail for Lydia. It contained a "next of kin memorial plaque" in memory of Josiah, sent by the Colonial Secretary. Lydia paused solemnly before lifting the so-called "Dead Man's Penny" out of its box. "Oh! my darling Joey. This is all I have left of you." The plaque was a substantial piece, cast in bronze, bearing an image of Britannia holding a trident and standing with a lion. Holding the weight of the medallion in her hand, Lydia was suddenly moved to take hold of her own fate.

That's it! she said to herself. No more shame and secrets. I want to honour Joey for who he really was. When she answered the Colonial Secretary, acknowledging receipt of the memorial plaque, she drew a big breath, divested herself of the pantomime (sister) and boldly signed, in her neat Methodist college script, "Lydia Powell (mother)."

Whale Song

I'd been out walking. Night was falling and I was still out there, musing on the lookout bench, watching the sunset, pink light on the hills.

Baleine was serene. Stars twinkling above the harbour, church spires dark against the indigo sky. Perfect outport beauty, I thought. But the town had given itself over to tourism, fancy paint jobs on the houses, lattes available in snazzy little cafes. I looked down the dark bay. Just to think, the fishery here is a thing of the past. The cod have diminished, gone out of the sea. A huge catastrophe created by human greed.

I'd come to Baleine with my women friends for a book club retreat at the well-appointed Bay Inn. All very nice, to have such upscale accommodation, but I couldn't help but feel nostalgic, grieving the loss of the outport life I'd known as a child visiting my grandparents in Totnes, a little cove across the strait from Baleine, where my ancestors had been settled for generations.

The night before, we'd had dinner in the dining room at the inn. "Oh, Mary, stop being such a hopeless romantic," my friend Barb said to me over mussels in white wine. "Outport life was rough. Haven't you read all those books with titles like *No Beautiful Shore?*"

Part of the package at the inn was a whale watching tour. I wasn't sure what I thought about people whizzing around the bay in a Zodiac, hoping for the thrill of seeing a whale. "Doesn't all that human gaping disturb the creatures?" I said. "Haven't we done enough damage already?"

Barb was on my case again. "Mary, Mary, you and your constant campaigning. Can't you relax and have a good time? Ever since your divorce you've been intense beyond."

My divorce. Already five years since Charlie had dumped me for that young Sherrie. Summarily dropped me off the cliff and left me to recover on the rocks below. Overnight, I went from being his "brown-eyed beauty with the champagne curls" to his ex-wife. I swore I'd never go near another man. But over time I adjusted, started dating and eventually met Craig.

I lingered on that bench, watching the blood red sun melt into the ocean, thinking about Craig. He wouldn't do. Mundane was the word that came to mind when I thought of him. Might as well face it—all those comfy snuggles in his restored Southcott house in the "heritage quarter" didn't cut it for me anymore.

Bitter. That's the word my therapist threw at me. She was right. I might be a hopeless romantic about outport Newfoundland, but I was still bitter about life. It was a strong, true feeling, defined and clean, like those tart little limes I tasted on my post-divorce trip to Peru—so tart they make your eyes water when you suck on them. *Quillabamba*, they call them.

"Don't let the bitterness blind you," the therapist had said. "You should try to leave those feelings behind and find joy in the world."

"Joy?" I said, dismissively.

"Start out with some good self-reflection," she continued. Have you ever thought about your part in the breakup of your marriage?"

As soon as she said that, I knew what my part was. Stubbornness. Refusal to admit, give in, be wrong.

Charlie and I lived a mostly peaceful life. There were no kids to worry about and we had a lot in common—two English teachers, bookworms, with a love of the outdoors, hiking, skiing. But sometimes, Charlie would lose his temper with me. "You can be a real vault, Mary. Closed shut. Unmovable." And I guess he was right. I do have a way of shutting down and sticking to my guns. For years I couldn't bring myself to speak to his brother, Jack, because of the way he treated his wife. Even though Jack repented and reformed, it took me a long time to "come down off my high horse," as Charlie said.

Tossing and turning in the tortured nights after Charlie moved out, I wondered if we would be still together if I'd been a little more open. But then again, when he announced he was leaving me, I did open my heart and I'd even begged. "Please don't throw away the life we built together." Broken and humiliated, I could see by the way he sat on the edge of his chair that our house was no longer his home, and no amount of openness on my part would stop him from returning to the arms of the delectable young Sherrie.

As the last streak of red on the horizon darkened to purple, I rose from the lookout bench, only to hear footsteps on the path behind me. I turned, peering through the waning light.

There in the gloaming stood George Hale. At the sight of him, adrenaline coursed through my body. As he approached the bench, I saw the glimmer of a tear in his eye. I'd forgotten how utterly handsome he was and how attracted to him I'd been—his fine features and smooth brown skin, his silky black ponytail, his broad shoulders. Right there on that hill in Baleine, he had the same immediate sensual, heart-gripping effect on me as he'd had five years before.

We'd met out on Cape Verde Island in Notre Dame Bay. He'd been doing carpentry work at the B&B where I was staying, and I was trying to hike off the after effects of divorce. A deaf man, George was full of charm and a master communicator, using his hands expressively as he signed. With his bubbling life force and uncanny ability to tune into people, he could hold the attention of a whole dinner table, while his wife, Judy, interpreted. A cheerful, devoted woman, Judy was crazy about her husband. And who could blame her? As I listened to her relay George's stories, I fixed my eyes on his face and couldn't help but wonder if she was capturing the nuances and undercurrents of what he was saying.

Flirting with the handsome carpenter was the last thing on earth I'd planned for that therapeutic hiking trip, but something pulsed between us. I remembered some sign language from a teaching stint at the School for the Deaf, so although there were always other people around, George and I found ways to commune. I remember having the sensation that my blood was heating up. I tried to curb myself—you've got to stop this romantic nonsense—but to no avail. Before I knew it, I was entertaining negative thoughts about George's marriage, how his wife wasn't at his level, didn't understand the sensitive poetic soul that I was discovering in him: the nature lover, the outport man with noble values.

In the end, we only ever managed to be alone once, out on the veranda. I was so moved by being close to him that I broke out of my normally strict privacy and showed him a poem I'd been writing about the island. "This place of flint and fog. My divinity." So much for curbing the romantic urges.

"You see the beauty I see," he signed, taking my hand into his big, warm hand. Sitting there with him on that summer's evening, I got a sense of how he felt the world, as we played a pointing game, each using their free hand to indicate something of beauty—the dark cloud bank on the horizon, the crab apple tree leaning against the old shed, the fading streaks of colour in the rock face. When the dinner bell rang, I was loath to take my hand out of his.

The next day, guilt-laden for flirting with someone else's husband, I kept picturing his adoring wife, how hurt she would be if she knew. Resolved to do the right thing, I took a big breath, packed my bags and left George behind on the island.

And now, here he was, large as life, in the Baleine moonlight. He smiled, then pointed to the rising moon, pulling us back in that hand-holding moment on the porch in Cape Verde.

I jumped up and started signing to him. The gestures came with ease, as I'd recently completed a refresher course in sign language that, uncannily, the lingering memory of George had prompted me to take. "How are you? What are you doing in Baleine?" I asked.

"Watching the moon," he signed back, brimming with mirth. "Watching you."

And with that, despite my bitter soul, I was instantly back where I'd been five years before. Smitten.

As we made our way down the pathway, George put his hand on my shoulder, lightly. Protective. When we reached the entrance to the inn, he steered me into the bar. We sat in the corner by the fireplace, ordered two glasses of wine and took up where we'd left off.

George slipped a notepad out of his shirt pocket and wrote: "I've been working on renovations here at the hotel. How about you?"

Hooking my index fingers together, I signed, "With friends for the weekend." Then I slid my thumb and index finger up my ring finger, to pose the awkward question that had been in my mind all the way down the path from the lookout. "Is your wife with you?"

George shuffled in his chair, sighed, then wrote *at home*, rather than the single magical word I was hoping for: *divorced*.

I took a large gulp of wine and tried to maintain my composure. Part of me was devastated by the news that he was still not a free agent, and the other part was glowing from the pleasure of sitting with him by the fire.

At that very moment, my book club buddies entered the bar, along with the innkeeper, Hugh Sampson.

"This looks cosy," said my brazen friend Barb, walking towards our table.

George stood up and shook hands with her and the other three girls, inviting them to sit with us. I noticed that he didn't as much as glance in Hugh Sampson's direction. The innkeeper greeted us and headed for the bar.

Then it was all wine quaffing and conviviality, with me interpreting for George, as his wife Judy had done out on Cape Verde. Once again, he took over the table, telling stories of the old Baleine he had known as a child on summer visits to his favourite uncle. Watching the loving way he spoke of his time with his old uncle—the early morning trips out the bay to the nets, the glory of the sunrises, the smell of the water, the camaraderie of *the men working together on the skiffs—reminded me of what* made me fall for him in the first place. There was a goodness to him, something truly noble. Not to mention his exotic good looks and the irresistible sensitivity around the eyes.

Get a grip, girl, I kept saying to myself, nothing's changed, he's a married man. Copious hours of therapy had not erased my bitterness about men cheating on their wives. But I felt an unspoken connection with George—something pulsated between the two of us and there was no denying it. He reached under the table and took my hand. Despite my misgivings, I held his hand, loving the closeness, he and I with our little complicity.

My friends too, were transfixed, held rapt by George's reminiscing. Then, uninvited, Hugh Sampson came over and sat down with us. Ignoring the mixture of talk and signing we were all enjoying, he promptly plonked his muscly forearms on the table and held forth, excluding George.

"Now ladies, I'll be taking you out in the bay tomorrow to see the whales. You're going to have the experience of a lifetime." A smooth-talking man with a resonant actor's voice and a St. John's brogue, he didn't seem to notice at all that he'd interrupted our bonhomie with George. He was definitely the barge-in-and-take-over type. Margot, the lawyer in our group, had told me about his fabled wheelings and dealings. Recently, he'd bought the Bay Inn for a song because the owner was dying. He soon got the business up and running but was paying his employees miserable salaries. Needless to say, the good folk of Baleine didn't have a good word for him.

"Those humpbacks are smart creatures, you know," continued Sampson, commanding our attention. "They can send out signals to find out where the capelin are." He had had a few beers and was feeling no pain. "Humpbacks emit scientific pings into the water. They're like radar machines." He paused, looking pleased with himself. "That's how they hunt. It's called *echolocation*."

George frowned and started signing. I jumped in with the interpreting, as dutiful as his wife. "George says it's not simple signals, there's nothing machine-like about whales," I explained, watching the little flame of anger in George's black eyes. "Humpbacks sing long, complex songs. There's a lot of communication going on between them. Synchronization. They send vibrating sound waves through the ocean. The singing goes on for hours. They emit all kinds of sounds, moans and whines, some with very high decibels. And the songs change."

I paused. "Just imagine, they sing to each other. What a thought! We'll never fathom the mystery of it all."

Hugh Sampson put his beer glass down. "Oh, come on now, there's no operas going on out there," he declared dismissively. "I wouldn't look for such great mystery. Its all about the rule of the wild—a simple matter of catching your prey."

George twitched, waved his hand as if to put an end to the conversation and went back to sipping his wine.

Hugh continued with authority. "Now, the whales haven't been in the bay the last few days. That can be explained by the fact that the capelin are way out at sea."

George couldn't help himself and jumped in again. I interpreted. "Capelin are diminishing, like the cod. All because of overfishing. The whales have less and less food to eat. That's why it's not so easy to find them in the bays anymore. It's sad, really."

I must admit I glowed with admiration as I spoke his words. This was a man after my own heart.

"But don't worry, the whales will back be in the bay tomorrow," pronounced Hugh, over-riding George's intervention. "So for sure, we'll go ahead with the excursion in the morning. There'll be you four women and another couple from away who are coming in late tonight. And there's one empty space due to a cancellation."

Barb jumped in, "Oh! let's invite George." An adept lip reader, George responded directly to the invitation by shrugging his shoulders and shaking his head. But the girls were insistent.

"Great, it's decided," said Barb. "What a merry crew we'll be!"

Hugh Sampson's eyes looked hard. Not merry at all.

That night, George followed me to my little attic room at the back of the inn—my invitation unspoken, implicit—and we finally consummated our long-standing desire for each other. There was no first time awkwardness. We kissed and touched with the intimacy and naturalness of a trusting couple. Our lovemaking was silent and so tender that I cried and cried. In that moment, my bitterness dissipated. I let myself flow into that inexplicable, visceral connection I'd had with this man from the second I'd laid eyes on him. George cried too.

Then he laughed. "Why are we crying? This is a gift, a wonderful turn of events."

Overwhelmed with emotion, naked and vulnerable, I shifted away, closing myself down.

He reached out, signed, "Stay with me. Please stay close."

I pulled the sheet around myself. "George, I can't ignore the fact that you're a married man. It's hard for me to get beyond that."

He shrugged his shoulders. "I thought we just got beyond that," he signed.

"It's not that simple, George, and you know it."

He grimaced, then continued signing. "I'm unhappy in my marriage. I know you know that. There's a huge divide between me and my wife. Her dream is to get ahead, buy a house in a new sub-division in Gander, live near a shopping centre. She thinks outports are backward places. But I want to go back home to Cape Verde, renovate my family's old house, settle down in the beauty and tranquility of the island."

So I had been right: George's wife was insensitive to her husband's deepest needs, and for that matter, he to hers. They were a bad match. I couldn't help but confront the truth. "How could you have married someone with such a different set of values?" I asked, almost accusingly. "You have such deep convictions and you're so sure about what you want."

He turned away from my bluntness, then looked back at me with tremendous sadness in his eyes. "I'm indebted to Judy. She's helped me so much. It hasn't been easy for me."

I was touched by his confession but couldn't stop my bitterness from coming to the fore. "Don't forget, I've met your Judy. Seen how crazy she is about you. I can't just overlook that. No matter how you look at it, marriage is a commitment and you're cheating on your wife. In fact, we're cheating on your wife."

George groaned and placed his fist on his chest, telling me how guilty he felt about Judy. Then his hands flew as he signed. "You're the only person I've ever confessed all this to. The only person I've ever cheated with. I feel so close to you. I've never forgotten you. The truth is, despite the fact that Judy is totally devoted to me, I've been lonely for years in my marriage."

With his confession of loneliness, my defences crumbled. I hadn't intended on letting George stay for the night. It's nothing, just a little fling, I'd justified to myself as we climbed the stairs to my room. But this was no little fling.

George took me back into his arms. He seemed sincere, sure of himself. Everything about him, even the clean, outdoorsy, woodsy smell of him, was pulling me in.

And we did have our night of love. But still, my stubborn scruples held me back. There was a sharpness to our loving. It made my eyes sting, like that little Peruvian lime.

In the morning, we took our coffee up the path to the lookout. It was a sunny, coolish July day but no wind—a gift, in this land. Gazing out over the morning bay, George signed, "I won't be here in Baleine for much longer. I've completed the work at the inn. Things didn't go well with Hugh Sampson."

I teased him, "You're such a hothead! This is the same thing that happened to you at the hotel on Cape Verde. I remember *how you and the owner were at daggers drawn.*"

George scribbled on his notepad, fast and furious, and handed it to me. "I insist on doing things well and I never ask for more than I deserve. Sampson tried to tell me how to do my job, cut corners. Now he doesn't want to pay me properly for my work. This man is a fake. He doesn't really know about the whales. He's a former radio announcer, a fast-talking townie who grew up on the asphalt, has no sense of nature. He's just talking off the top of his head. My childhood buddy, Ely Bennett, who lives here, drives the boat for him on the whale tours. He says Sampson spews out made-up science for the tourists."

When we got back to the inn, we found my friends at the breakfast table, chatting with the young couple who had arrived late the night before, Gemma and Nigel from Manchester, England. Nigel, a square-faced young man with ruddy cheeks, was all talk.

"This is our 'oneymoon," he announced with his Coronation Street accent. "The dream of a lifetime, to go whale watching."

His bride, looking pale and drawn, sat shivering in her chair: her off-the-shoulder frilly blouse more suitable for honeymooning in the Caribbean than in Notre Dame Bay. The poor girl was definitely not living the dream of a lifetime. She drew a wool sweater around her shoulders. "I'm here for Nigel," she said, yawning and looking at her husband admiringly.

What kind of blind love is this? I thought to myself. An English city girl forced to go whale watching in the wilds of Newfoundland on her honeymoon.

"We're a little tired," said Nigel. "You see, we were married just two days ago. Yesterday we had to catch a connection to Heathrow and fly across the Atlantic to St. John's. Then we had to drive all the way out here. A bit of a rush, I'm afraid. But I could only take one week off from my job." He beamed at us proudly, "I'm assistant manager of a Tesco supermarket." Gemma was beaming too.

Well, each to his own, I thought. You might as well admire your husband if you're going to have one.

A few minutes later, we were all trundling out the door of the hotel, laden with hats and binocs, cameras and wind jackets. George tried to slip away but Barb hooked his arm and dragged him along with our merry crew.

Hugh Sampson was waiting on the wharf, dressed in a jaunty sailing jacket. "Fine day for whales," he said in his baritone voice, "I'm feeling optimistic we'll find them."

George's old friend Ely Bennett was at the wheel of the boat. He caught George's eye. "Hello there, buddy," he called, giving his friend a welcome wave. "George will be a good one to have along," he said cheerfully to Hugh. "He knows this arm of the bay well. We fished along this shore with his uncle when we were youngsters."

Hugh turned his shoulders and got busy with the ropes.

The inevitable wind had come up and the Zodiac, still moored at the dock, was already heaving with the chop of the waves. George helped the girls onto the boat. Then Nigel, laden with gigantic camera lenses, jumped clumsily on board, leaving his terrified young bride to step off the dock on her own. It was George who came to her rescue, helping her into a seat next to me, where she sat tenuously. The engine started up and we zoomed out into bay.

Now it was the chill of the Atlantic on our faces, the sharp smell of spruce from the land, the vastness of the open bay with the vista of islands in the distance. George and I exchanged glances and he took my hand. My book club buddies, singing and skylarking, winked at me with delight. I was feeling whisked away, thrilled and full of misgivings all at the same time. Holding hands like a teenager, I said to myself. What am I up to? What if George's Judy could see the two of us?

The further we went out the bay, the stiffer the wind and the cooler the air. I looked across at Gemma. She was clinging for dear life to the ropes on the Zodiac. We were banging over some fairly hefty waves now, Gemma cringing and closing her eyes with each thrust.

"Are you alright?" I shouted over the wind.

"Not really," she whimpered. I could only imagine what a shock to the senses this was for a girl from Manchester.

"Hang on tight!" I told her. "There's no danger. The driver knows what he's doing."

"I've never been out in a boat before," she said, widening her terrified eyes. "I'm doing this for Nigel, you see." Her Nigel was in the front with Hugh and Ely. It was all camera clicks and male talk up there. Hugh was explaining about the whales. He kept pointing in this direction and that, as Ely wheeled the boat around.

George was watching the men, getting that steely look in his eyes again. He let go of my hand long enough to sign to me. "Whales need silence. They communicate by vibration, oscillations. Their songs travel on sound waves. All our whizzing around only disturbs them, confuses them. No wonder Sampson can't find them."

Now the fog was upon us. A long, thick bank of it was rolling into the bay. Within minutes, we were enveloped. "Don't worry about the fog," shouted Hugh over the whirr of the engine, "That will never stop a whale from feeding." And on we went, speeding into this inlet and that one, roaring around headlands that you could just decipher through the mist.

George's face was now bearing a permanent frown. He glanced at Hugh, then he placed two fingers in the shape of a V on his forehead—the easily recognizable sign for stupid. I laughed, pressing close to him.

The girls had been singing and animated but as time wore on, with no sign of whales and chilled by the fog, their energy was draining. "I think the whales are after goin' over to Twillingate for their lunch, Mr. Sampson," said Barb, in her usual droll manner. "We're all a bit wind-beaten and ready to go home."

Nigel turned and looked daggers at us. He'd come all the way from Manchester to the ends of the earth to see whales and had no intention of abandoning the expedition. Gemma, still hanging desperately onto the ropes and shuddering with the cold, gave me a pleading look. She wanted her Nigel to have his day. The fog was so thick now you couldn't see anything at all. "Let's not give up yet" said Hugh, slapping his new-found friend Nigel on the back. "We could see a whale any minute now." So on we went, roaring around in the whiteness with no inkling of where we were.

Suddenly, George let go of my hand and stood up. He stepped over the seats and grabbed Hugh by the arm, pointing excitedly, grunting and indicating that we should go back into the inlet we'd just left. Hugh's immediate reaction was to shake his head and refuse to turn the boat around. George was insistent.

Finally, Ely said to Hugh, "He knows about whales, Mr. Sampson. Deaf people can feel their pressure waves, vibrations in the water."

"Sounds like a pile of nonsense to me," said Hugh, "but alright, you can turn around and give it one more try."

As the boat turned, there was a break in the fog and a patch of rich blue sky appeared. Then we heard the unmistakable wheeze of a whale blow, like air bursting out of a gigantic balloon. A minute later, just like that, a humpback breached out of the water only 20 feet away, right in front of us. A private show. The sight of the mammoth creature as he heaved himself up into the air triggered something in our primal selves. Elated, we hooped and hollered as the whale came down, slapping and splashing.

"Bloody Hell!" shouted Nigel as he scrambled to focus his biggest lens, click! click! click! Then immediately, the whale was up in the air again, even closer this time, sea water streaming off its body, mouth wide open, giving us a whiff of its intensely foul fishy breath.

"I told you this would be the thrill of a lifetime," shouted Hugh, taking full credit for the show.

A glorious beam of sunlight cut through, dissipating the fog. Gemma smiled, her eyes brimming with tears. "I'm so happy for Nigel. It's a blessing," she pronounced. "It's a blessing for our marriage."

I turned to George, warm sunshine on my shoulders. "You sensed the whale was there," I signed. "It's beautiful how you feel the world, George."

The whale breached one last time and as the boat tilted on the waves, George slid against me. "This one's ours, Mary," he signed. His eyes filled with mirth, "a blessing for you and me?"

I nodded, unhindered, no sting in my eyes. Joy.

Honour Silence

St. John's was a far cry from the Tudor village perfection of Ashington. The battered old capital of Newfoundland was a greasy port, with steep hills, higgly-piggly houses, brash locals, rough north winds and bracing sea air.

But in the staffroom at Graham's College for Girls, where the teachers drank tea, smoked cigarettes and discussed their work, Vera felt like she'd never left England. It was the very claustrophobia she'd tried to flee—they'd carried it across the Atlantic, intact.

So much for my North American adventure, she said to herself. I see how it works: The teachers come out on their colonial mission, live in their ex-pat bubble, then go back home when they retire. It's as if they never truly arrived here!

Vera noticed how the little Graham's girls walked past the staffroom door with trepidation, feeling the level of command and control emanating from inside.

"Do we have to scare the girls like that?" she remarked to her roommate Millicent (Miss Blane). "Surely that's not necessary!"

"It's a matter of keeping composure," insisted Millicent, a young woman in her late twenties like Vera, but already slavishly set in her ways. "We can't have a free-for-all. Our girls must behave impeccably."

In the lesson plan meetings, Vera despaired once again. The imperial mission to St. John's was being taken very seriously:

from Guy Fawkes to the Spanish Armada, the curriculum barely touched on anything outside of Britain.

She looked out the window of the old clapboard building where Graham's was housed. The view of St. John's harbour and the imposing Signal Hill was stunning.

"What about Newfoundland history?" she dared ask at a meeting, only in her second week there. "I've been reading about the battles between the French and English for possession of St. John's harbour. This is a centuries-old strategic port."

Miss Mandly, the headmistress, was quick to bring Vera into line. "We're here to follow the British curriculum," she said, narrowing her eyes. Vera could feel from the chill in Miss Mandly's voice that she had never, even for a second, pondered Signal Hill and its rich history.

"With regard to culture and curriculum," persisted Vera boldly, "I've been studying Stuart Hall and other young writers in the *Left Review*. The new thinking as we approach the 1960s is that teachers should help students appreciate their own culture, so they feel proud to be who they are. Very innovative, don't you think?"

Colleagues around the table drew back in astonishment. For a moment, even Miss Mandly was stuck for words, but she quickly rallied and gave Vera an amused smile.

"Sounds interesting, I'm sure, but we still have a lot of basic literacy work to do with these girls."

It was a sunny September. Vera walked the streets of St. John's, marvelling at the light on the surrounding hills and enjoying the smiles and greetings she received from the locals.

"From England, are you?" said a forthright woman at a bus stop on Water Street, when she heard Vera's plummy accent. "We're used to seeing Englishmen around here, for one reason or the other. Our government was even taken over by Britain during the Depression, you know."

"Yes, I read about that," said Vera. "How did it go?"

"Those were hard times—the Brits did some good things, I s'pose but if you don't mind me saying, they talked down to us and stirred up a lot of ire. My husband worked in the government at the time. He had an English boss who even had the nerve to correct his accent! Jim used to come home from work fuming."

Vera's mind went to Miss Mandly and her cohort of cultural missionaries, overriding local culture as a matter of principle. "I'm sorry to hear that but I'm not surprised. We're hoping for change in Britain now. There's a political movement to get rid of that old ruling elite."

"Well good luck with that one," retorted the woman. "They'd be a hard crowd to root out."

Vera laughed. "Yes indeed, they can be very difficult to 'root out' as you say."

Riding up Casey Street on the bus, Vera looked out the window at the row houses tumbling down the hill and thought, I'm beginning to like this place.

Vera was also enjoying her pupils, their lively way, their lilting accent. But as she'd suspected, tales of moody English moors, thatched roofed cottages and stately manor houses hardly resonated in the minds of these little Newfoundland girls.

This is simply unfair, thought Vera. These children never get to articulate anything about their own world.

Then she came up with an idea. "Girls, you are to write a piece about St. John's. That will be your homework this week. Something you know and care about." And in came the assignments: little compositions and poems, all written with fountain pens in British cursive script, all abounding with images of the endless winter, the precious summer. One girl wrote a poem about a crackling bonfire on a rocky beach, another described the joys of sliding down the snowy hills in winter.

"A rather novel idea," said Grace Wilson, the history teacher, at tea break in the staffroom. A prim little woman with fine features and short-cropped hair, Miss Wilson never hesitated to speak her mind. "But don't forget, we must ensure that we teach 'the canon.' I can tell you, these pupils need solid preparation for the exams." Miss Wilson's eyes were full of stern belief—she meant well—this was a duty she was determined to carry out.

"The girls in my class are thrilled to learn the classic British songs," piped up Miss Jones, the mild-mannered Welsh music teacher. Vera could see pride and pure devotion in her eyes, too.

Miss Jones' choir had performed "Rule Britannia" for the school assembly the day before. Vera couldn't help but be impressed by the sight of the bright-eyed little girls, decked out in their serge tunics, singing the great patriotic anthem in perfect three-part harmony, descant and all: "Rule Britannia, Britannia rule the waves, Britons never never never shall be slaves."

"Your pupils are excellently trained," Vera told Miss Jones, "but I hear that there is a rich tradition of music here. The girls could be singing some of the local songs as well."

"Surely goodness, that would be more suitable in their own homes," said Miss Wilson.

Vera gave an impertinent shrug of her shoulders. She knew what she was up against. I'm never going to fit in at Graham's, she thought. Here I am again, the awkward one, going against the tide. Story of my life.

Weekends were long, full of lesson plans and marking. By November, winter had moved in with inclement weather, and Vera was mostly stuck in the apartment with Millicent. Millie did go out occasionally in the evenings, rather furtively, Vera thought. Where could she be going? The teachers didn't seem to have much of a social life. Millie was pleasant enough, but seemed short on ideas. Being the gym mistress, she mostly devoted her time to cleaning her white trainers, starching her gym blouses and pressing her pleated wool skirt.

"Next week I'm teaching the girls Scottish country dancing," she said to Vera cheerily. "It can be quite tricky, you know, but we'll get there by dint of hard work!"

On Sundays, the teachers dutifully marched off to church in the dankness of the Anglican Cathedral, nodding and giving little half-smiles to fellow parishioners, including Graham's girls, who, once sighted by the teachers, made sure they were sitting up ramrod straight—good deportment was a much-touted principle at the school. Graham's pupils were ever watchful of encountering a teacher in church or on a street in town: if seen chewing gum, dropping a candy wrapper on the ground or committing some other sin that "let the school down," they could expect to be singled out at Monday morning assembly.

On Sunday evenings, Vera went along with the teachers to Miss Wilson's place, a drafty walk-up apartment in a Victorian house in the grander part of town on Circular Road. Glass of sherry in hand, they sat around a shortwave radio and listened to the BBC overseas news.

The Suez Canal crisis was in full bloom. Vera was not surprised to see her colleagues shaking their heads in agreement with Anthony Eden and his Conservative sidekicks. "The Labour Party's attack on the prime minister is nothing short of disgraceful!" proclaimed Grace Wilson in a huff.

Predicable, thought Vera. If they knew I campaigned for Labour, I'd be shunned. They'll cling to the old class system till their dying day.

"Yes, you're ever so right, Grace," gushed Miss Blane to Miss Wilson, cocking her head in admiration. "Labour doesn't work in the nation's best interest."

Vera had noticed that outside of school, the teachers mostly dropped the "Miss" salutation and resorted to first names, although the switching pattern between the use of first and surnames in the group was not always easy to navigate. Unable to resist a little goading, she chimed in with: "Nonetheless, Grace,

I did read that Labour is on the rise. You may be surprised by the results of the next election."

Christmas came and the Graham's teachers were invited to a Christmas Eve do at the Anglican Bishop's manse. Most of them had one dressy outfit for such occasions, involving a tweed skirt and wool sweater set and some sort of brooch to fancy themselves up. Vera had a baggy dress that she tried to press. It still came out looking shapeless, but, with a yen to look dapper, she draped an Isadora Duncan-style scarf over her shoulder and went off to the Anglican manse.

"Come in and have some Christmas cheer!" said Bishop Heath, a handsome man with dark eyes and bushy eyebrows. Puffing away at a cigarette, he welcomed the group of teachers heartily, even touching them on the shoulders and patting them on the back, making Margot (Miss Jones) laugh nervously and blush beet red.

Vera accepted a rather stiff gin and tonic from the Bishop and soon found herself engaged in what seemed to her a flirtatious conversation with the attractive clergyman. She noticed her heart rate was up a little. Life had been so dull since she'd arrived in St. John's. She'd seen how lively and spirited the locals were but had not been able to break free of the coterie of teachers and their earnest intentions.

The Bishop was eager to know what plays she was teaching in English class. "I'm a bit of a thespian, you see." Vera was lapping up the male attention, but she did notice the other teachers glancing her way as she accepted a refill of the G and T.

"I did quite a lot of amateur theatre back in Ashington," she said, flicking her scarf and feeling surprisingly at ease. "There's nothing like the challenge of stepping onto the boards."

The Bishop swished the ice in his drink. "You should join our local group, the St. John's Players. We're starting rehearsal for Noel Coward's *Blithe Spirit* in the new year."

After Christmas, (overcooked turkey and water-logged vegetables at Miss Jones' and Miss Thomas' house) it was back to school. The January weather was a real challenge—icy sidewalks and mile-high snowbanks.

In the first staff meeting of the year, Miss Wilson raised the issue of a Grade V student, Deborah McKnee, who'd been displaying defiant behaviour—falling out of the line on the way to assembly, turning up for physical education without her gym bloomers and, most seriously, not wearing the correct uniform blouse (imported Manchester white cotton).

"You're ever so right to bring this up, Grace," said Miss Blane, in perpetual admiration. "That girl never turns up properly equipped for gym class."

Deborah McKnee was an enthusiastic student in Vera's English class. She earned top marks for her poem about being lonely until she met her friend the snowman who eventually melted away, leaving his cap as a keepsake.

Vera had, in fact, noticed that Deborah in no way achieved the level of discipline of most Graham's pupils, who followed the rules with amazing precision: they'd learned to take pride in their school and recognized that it was a privilege to become a little British girl right in the middle of downtown St. John's. But Deborah seemed to take a total miss on the Graham's pride. She simply didn't have it in her. As well, she was a little pale and not always neatly coiffed. Vera had wondered what kind of home life she had.

Bracing herself, Vera stood up to Grace Wilson.

"Those uniform blouses are expensive. I was told that the Royal Stores on Water Street has to import them from England, just for Graham's girls. Maybe Deborah McKnee's parents can't come up with that kind of money."

Miss Mandly intervened. "We can't allow exceptions to the rules. The girls must learn the importance of absolute discipline. That is what Graham's is all about. I'll look into the matter and we'll take it up again at the next meeting."

"Maybe we could have a word with the McKnee girl's parents," added Miss Hornby, who had by far the softest touch of any of the teachers.

A myopic woman with thick glasses and a sunny smile, Jane Hornby taught Mathematics and Latin. Vera had noticed her East End London accent and learned about her modest background when they went to the Capitol Theatre together to see the new film of *The Importance of Being Earnest*. Afterwards, they had tea back at Jane's place.

Sensing that Jane's lowly origins made her more empathetic than the other colleagues, and desperate for an ally in her plight to humanize Graham's, Vera tried to engage her in criticism of the overly strict regime at the school.

"Don't you think we could lighten up on some of the rules? After all, Graham's isn't a military academy!"

For a brief moment, Jane's eyes flickered, and she looked like she was about to agree with Vera. But then, shaking her shoulders, she corrected herself. "We were sent out here for a reason, you know. We do represent our queen and country. It's a question of professional honour."

Vera turned her head away, trying not to roll her eyes. She'd given up on the concept of "honour" a long time ago.

***

"This will be the making of you, darling," Mum had said when eight-year-old Vera was sent off to Manor Oak Academy. "Try to be more positive. It's generous of your father to pay for you to go to such a fine school."

End of term report cards from the academy ("refuses to fit in," "lacking in school spirit") soon indicated that the strict discipline of the upper-class institution was only serving to nurture Vera's growing rebellious instincts.

Vera always claimed that it was a school tradition known as "honour silence" that caused her premature departure from the hallowed halls of Manor Oak Academy. This was a form of discipline in which little girls were left in the classroom unsupervised for 30 minutes or even longer and instructed to sit absolutely still and in total silence while the teacher was absent. They had to remain immobilized at their desks, staring at the blackboard where HONOUR SILENCE was writ large.

Years later, Vera was still railing away about it to her mother. "You have no idea of the agony I suffered —a little child trying to keep still and not utter a sound, for what seemed like an eternity. And on top of that, there was the threat of betrayal and punishment: anyone who spoke or even moved an inch in their seat was to be reported on by her fellow students. And layered on top of all that was the shame. Breaking the silence constituted letting the school down. Letting *England* down. That's a terrible pressure to put on a child. I just couldn't stand it."

***

Now, here in St. John's, Vera had come across the same torturous practice.

"Graham's maintains some of the worst aspects of the British system—honour silence, for example," she'd said flatly to Jane Hornby. "There's nothing honourable about it."

"But it teaches self-mastery, Vera. Graham's alumnae testify that it's character forming and helped them succeed in life. Honour silence is a respected tradition."

How foolish of me to ever think I would find an ally at Graham's, thought Vera.

In mid-January, an Anglican missionary who had been working in Borneo, paid a visit to the school, accompanied by Bishop Heath. The missionary gave a talk to the girls about "less fortunate" children in the Empire who had been taught the virtues of Anglicanism and were now heading for a meaningful future.

After the talk, the Bishop brought the missionary, a rather befuddled man, balding and full of smiles, for tea in the staffroom. The teachers were quite titillated by the visit. Over the clinking of cups and British chatter, Vera found herself engaged once again by the bushy-browed and ever-lively Bishop. She felt delightfully at ease, as if speaking to an old friend.

"How is your acting coming along, Bishop Heath? I don't imagine they get too many Bishops in the amateur theatre scene."

"I am indeed the one and only clergyman in the troupe," said the Bishop, laughing. "And oh yes, that reminds me, Miss Portland... or may I call you Vera? You must come along to audition for our Noel Coward play, *Blithe Spirit*. You would really suit the role of Elvira, the hero's mischievous former wife. You definitely have the comic spirit to play that character."

The audition was held in the auditorium of Beade College, the Anglican boy's school just down the road from Graham's. It was a sleety Tuesday evening. Vera had considered not going out when she saw the freezing rain, but the Bishop had sparked her interest and, desperate to step outside of her Graham's life, she crumped her way over the slippery sidewalks and arrived late.

"So glad you could make it," said the Bishop, taking her coat. "Come right in now, you're actually up next. I've already auditioned for my part, Dr. Bradman, friend of Charles Condomine."

Vera was promptly called to the stage to read her lines as Elvira, who has come back as a ghost to haunt her former husband, Charles, and his second wife, Ruth. The cynical, carefree and naughty character of Elvira really appealed to Vera, and she'd spent some time preparing her part.

The actor playing the role of Charles Condomine immediately caught her attention. A stocky man with intense blue eyes, he shook her hand and put her at ease.

"Hi, I'm Dave. Pleasure to meet you," he said in a deep, smoky actor's voice. "Shall we get started? Vera, isn't it?"

Vera could see his eyes twinkling at her as she read her first line. Encouraged, she played her part with aplomb.

"You've been thoroughly churlish ever since I arrived, Charles. I want to cry but I don't think I can."

"Why do you want to cry?" intoned baritone Dave, winking at her outrageously.

Vera gave him a dramatic pout. "You've been so irascible."

Dave hammed it up, swooping his hand to his forehead, "I'm thinking of my poor wife, Ruth."

"To hell with Ruth!" retorted Vera with a glint in her eye.

By the end of the flirtatious encounter on the stage, Vera cheeks were stinging.

"I hear you're one of the British teachers down to Graham's," said Dave. "Quite the honour to have you on board." Vera noticed the teasing look on his face. "And a delight to work with you. You're such a good actor, Vera."

"Thank you but really, I'm only an amateur. You're the one who seems at ease with acting."

He gave Vera a big open smile. "A group of us are going to the Candlelite Restaurant for a late-night snack, why don't you come along?"

As Vera fumbled a few words about having to work in the morning, another woman came up to her. "Hi, I'm Delores, the director. Welcome to our humble players." Delores was petite and lively, with a jaunty Doris Day bob. "I hope you're coming to the Candlelite with us."

At the restaurant it was all laughter and chatting—effusive, fun and clever.

"Of course, all women long to play Elvira," said Delores. "And I can see that you have the spunk to play the part. Consider yourself in the production, my dear."

"Oh yes, you've definitely got it," said Dave. "The wicked English socialite." Vera was not used to such positive input. And such physical proximity—Dave was sitting next to her in the cozy Candlelite booth. She was aware of his hockey-playing muscularity, his shoulder brushing hers each time he made a jovial remark.

"What town was it that you came from in England? I bet it's all pretty and tranquil. Must be hard getting used to this rough old place!"

Later, at the unthinkable hour of midnight, she was glowing as she undid the latch to let herself into the apartment, trying not to wake Millicent. But sure enough, the gym mistress appeared in her hairnet and nightdress to greet her.

"I've been ever so concerned, Vera, what happened to you?"

"Oh, just rehearsing," said Vera with an irrepressible smile.

She lay awake that night. Dave, a perfect stranger whom she knew nothing about, not even his surname, had already gotten to her in a way no man ever had. Her relationships with men had been awkward—a squeeze or a kiss from a fellow actor after a few drinks in the pub, a stiff conversation on a blind date that never took off, and then a brief and perfunctory engagement to a local Labour party official before she fled England.

But she was drawn to Dave, and it seemed to be mutual. He'd even insisted on walking her home. They'd chatted quite naturally all the way, telling stories of their theatre experiences. Vera noticed that when it was just the two of them, he stopped the joking around and spoke in a thoughtful way, soliciting her opinion and truly attempting to have a conversation.

"It's interesting to hear your views on modern theatre, Vera. I can't make any inroads with my buddies in the St. John's Players. They're stuck in their ways."

"I couldn't agree more. It's high time we moved beyond Noel Coward."

When they got to Vera's door, he placed his hand lightly on her back and gave her a long look in the eye.

"It's great to meet you, Vera, I look forward to our next rehearsal."

Still awake in the wee hours, Vera worried that Dave was slightly shorter than her lanky self. And she would have to do something about her appearance. Her mother's admonitions on the subject came back to her.

"Look at the state of you, Vera. You should pay more attention, press your clothes. How will you ever succeed in life and catch a husband looking like that? You're not a bad-looking girl. Despite being tall, you have a nice figure, a good nose. But those wispy curls are a little too thin. You just need to get some form of perm. Don't frown at me, pet, I'm only thinking of your best interests."

That's what I'll do, said Vera to herself, resolving to go to sleep. I'll get a perm, spruce myself up.

At the next rehearsal, she was sporting her permed curls and had a good grip on her new lines, which she'd been practising hard. Dave had been practicing too. The scene went well. They both felt the serendipity. When they finished, Dave complimented her again on her acting.

"I like how you capture the farcical with the tragic," he said, still with that ironic look, and touching her elbow, making Vera felt lightheaded. He stayed close. "If you don't mind me saying, that's a great hairdo. You look fantastic."

Vera was overwhelmed. She cleared her throat. "You express Charles' ambivalence so subtly. That's not easy. You really portray how unsure Charles is about himself."

"Oh, that's not hard for me," said Dave with a chuckle. "It's been the story of my life, uncertainty... but you don't want to hear about that!"

He looked her straight in the eye again. "Anyway, sorry, but I've got to run off tonight, duty calls." He touched her hand. "See you next week? Maybe we can go to the Candlelite again."

Vera fretted as she walked home. What did Dave mean by "duty calls?" Have I got myself in another awkward situation? Is he married?

If that was the case, she couldn't bear the hypocrisy. Not after what happened with her own father.

***

"I won't accept your hypocritical life, Mum. Who do you think you're fooling?"

"Please, Vera darling, you must stop being an angry teenager and go along with the way things are."

"You want to live in this brick house behind the garden wall, playing the nicely turned-out wife of the greengrocer. Don't you think people know that Dad is living common-law over the store with another woman? He's a lady's man and a cheat but you still let him come for tea and run around after him when he needs you."

"You must curb your temper, dear. And you shouldn't say such things about your father. There's no need to be unkind."

"No need to be unkind? We look nothing but ridiculous, Mum, going along with Dad's scheme to have two wives. You let him get away with blue murder, but I'm expected to behave like little Miss Muffet. We live in the house like two little birds in a cage, for Dad to visit when the spirit moves him. And all you do is keep smiling. You can keep up appearances with your rose garden and custard puddings if you want, but not me."

***

At the Friday afternoon staff meeting, the topic of Deborah McKnee took centre stage. The girl was in serious trouble and not only for her lax demeanour and lack of school pride. Miss Wilson reported that young Deborah had jumped up from her desk and run into the corridor rather than respond to renewed queries about her uniform blouse. The girl had then had "some sort of crying fit" which was "most unbecoming."

There was talk of meeting with her father about the possibility of transferring the girl to another, (lesser) Anglican school, which "would be more suitable for her." St. Luke's, with its looser rules, polyester uniforms and local teachers, could be appropriate.

"But Deborah is bright and fits in very well in my English class," objected Vera, getting outraged. "She's quite good at writing poetry and enjoys the readings. Surely to goodness we can avoid a drastic measure like transferring her out of the school."

"But this is not the first of her crying fits," said Miss Mandly. "We've warned her father that she needs to settle down. He seems to think he knows something about education because he works for the government. But the poor girl is motherless and clearly has emotional problems. Graham's is obviously not the best place for her."

Vera stood up. "So rather than help, you're going to drum her out," she barked, heading for the door. "I won't be part of this."

"It's too bad," said kindly Miss Hornby, trying to counterbalance the hatchet-like decision. "But she may be happier in another school."

"That's right," said Miss Mandly, her eyes following Vera out the doorway. "I'll set the process in motion."

And with that, Deborah McKnee was out of Graham's.

That night, Vera stewed over the decision: I've had enough, I never should have come here, I don't belong, I might have known, now it's all come crashing down... again.

In the morning, she went to work weary and raw. As she hung her coat in the staff room, Grace Wilson came in. "Good morning, Vera," she said briskly. "I hope you've recovered from yesterday's emotions. It's all very unfortunate, but sometimes we have to make difficult decisions, for everyone's good."

"I don't think dismissing Deborah McKnee was for anyone's good," snapped Vera, fleeing the room. As she headed up the stairs to her classroom, it struck her: I can put up with a lot from these women, I know their little mentality so well, but this is downright cruelty. I don't think I can stick to my two-year contract with Graham's.

In the next few days, besides mulling over her future at the school, Vera turned her thoughts to seeing Dave again. The rehearsal was coming up. Was she being silly, with her new curls? Would he turn out to be a disappointment? She resolved to keep her cool. Above all, she did not want to get involved with a married man.

When she arrived at the auditorium, he was waiting for her by the door. She tried to act distant, but he came right up to her, touching her arm, as if assuming there was something between them. "Sorry I had to rush off the last time. I hope you can join me for a snack at the Candlelite later." He looked relaxed, available and open. Not at all the cheating villain Vera had been constructing in her mind.

With the sound of his voice and the touch of his hand, her resolve was fast melting. She consented awkwardly, falling into a plummy British polite response, that she hated herself for. "That's terribly kind of you, I am ever so appreciative, are you sure you have time this evening?"

Dave smiled and Vera noticed his dimples. "My pleasure," he said. "I've got all the time in the world."

It was a windy night with drifting snow. Most of the players were going directly home, so this time it was just the two of them. As they made their way up Long's Hill in a roaring gale, Dave put his arm around Vera's shoulder, joking, "I'm not trying to be fresh, just don't want you to get blown over."

Inside the warmth of the restaurant, Vera looked around and noticed several couples drinking wine, engaged in *tête-à-tête*, having what looked like a "dinner date." Her cheeks were stinging at the very thought of it.

Dave ordered a beer for himself, and Vera accepted a port. He immediately started chatting away. So friendly and direct. "I should tell you a bit about meself! Civil servant, working on policy in the Department of Education, for my sins. All kinds of adjustments to make since Confederation. It's only been six years; we're not very Canadian down here yet!"

Vera took a good look him. He was somewhat dishevelled—rusty brown curls uncombed, a tea stain on his shirt. Maybe in his mid-thirties? And so good-looking.

He reached his hand across the table, touching the tips of her fingers.

"It's nice to get to chat to you, Vera. I hope you don't mind me asking, but what ever possessed you to move to this god-forsaken corner of the world."

"I was looking for adventure. And getting away from England seemed like a good idea. So I applied to the 'Surplus Women' programme that finds jobs overseas for unemployed and unmarried women. And here I am. But to tell you the truth, Graham's feels mostly like I'm back home. Except for the students. They're a real treat. Lovely little girls."

Dave winced, ran his hand through his curls. "Well, it's time for me to fess up and tell you about my daughter Debbie—Deborah McKnee—she was in your poetry class."

Emotion raced through Vera. Good God! She'd been flirting with Deborah McKnee's father! She reached for her glass of port, knocking it over. "Oh dear, how clumsy of me…"

Dave mopped up the spilled port with his serviette and ordered a refill. "Sorry to surprise you like that, Vera. I wasn't sure how to handle this. My daughter told me all about you. Admires you so much. She says you're the girls' favourite teacher. You actually *like* them, take delight in them. They love you for it."

"Oh, my goodness! Is Deborah alright? I'm so sorry about how she was treated at Graham's."

"Not to worry. She's settling into her new school. I should have moved her out of Graham's a while ago. Those teachers kept calling me, and I kept telling them Debbie was more than able to keep up with their standards. You see, her mother died in childbirth, and I've done my best with her, but she's very independent. My sister Betty's been living with us, helping out, but she hasn't been able to get through to her. Debbie's headstrong and creative, not your average girl. I guess our house is kind of unconventional."

"I know how smart your Deborah is. I really wanted to keep her as a student."

"I was hoping she'd bloom down to Graham's. But quite the opposite happened. Those teachers are a hard-hearted crowd. They almost drove her into the ground. She just couldn't fit into their mould. And they wouldn't give her a chance. Nothing but pure elitism."

"You're ever so right. You know, as I child, I never fit into the mould at school either. I really appreciate how Deborah felt at Graham's. And I was very cross with the way my colleagues treated her."

"Well, they can't help who they are, I suppose. They like to keep a firm handle on things. Control trumps creativity in their books!" Dave smiled and lightened things up. "I was damned if I was going to lay out the money for that fancy white blouse from England. I think that really got their goat!"

Vera laughed. "Yes, indeed. They don't like to be defied. Especially by a lowly parent." She sipped her port, feeling the bliss of their shared complicity and the relief that Dave had no wife to cheat on.

Suddenly, the closeness between the two of them increased one hundredfold. They leaned towards each other across the Candlelite table with its little lamp and individual juke box.

"You're a lovely woman, Vera. Don't let those colleagues of yours get to you."

"Well, I've been thinking about that for a while now. I'm simply not suited to Graham's. There's lots of surplus women in England who could come over and take my place."

Vera paused, looking pleased with herself. "So I've arranged to see our friend Bishop Heath next week. I'm going to ask him to speak to the Board about giving me a transfer. Next year, I may well follow your Debbie to St. Luke's, where I'm told the rules are more relaxed and there's no snootery. That would jolly well suit me."

Dave raised his glass. "Well, that will *jolly well* suit me too. You're getting out of that straight jacket at Graham's. And you're sticking around St. John's." He took Vera's hand. "Shall I play us a tune? Do you like Johnny Mathis?"

"Sounds wonderful," said Vera. She had no idea who Johnny Mathis was.

Dave crooned to "Until the Twelfth of Never."

There was a blast of cold air as the door opened and two people entered the restaurant. Vera could not believe her eyes. It was Miss Wilson and Miss Blane. Was this where Millie went on her furtive nights out? As they removed their snowy scarves and hats, they caught sight of Vera, ensconced in a cosy booth, holding hands with the handsome Dave. Vera nodded a casual hello to the two wide-eyed women.

Then she thought victoriously: Now I feel like I've truly arrived in St. John's. And I think I'm going to fit in here, very nicely.

Inchworm

Mrs. Hearn was scuffing around the kitchen in her felt slippers. She called up the stairwell.

"Jennifer! Theresa! You girls get down here and eat your breakfast. Your father wants you to be seen at early Mass."

She plopped the porridge into the cracked bowls. Another day of smoothing oil over troubled waters.

Out for his morning constitutional, Mayor Mickey Flynn almost lost his footing on his way down the slick incline of Patrick Street. He reached Water Street and headed down to the harbour, where he could get a good stride going and see what vessels were in. Docked in front of Bowring's was a French naval ship, in port on a courtesy call. Flynn cast his knowing eye up and down the length of her. Two French sailors were cleaning something off the side of the ship. An inveterate supervisor, he stopped to watch the men at work. If it wasn't for the language barrier, he'd be asking questions, handing out orders. The sailors were laughing and chatting as they threw buckets of water at the mess.

I bet I know what those Frenchmen are laughing about, he thought. Looks to me like someone threw up over the rail. They held a big party for the crowd at the university down here last night. Something about cultural exchange. "Culture, my eye," he muttered. "God only knows who was there and what went on. There'll be lots of hangovers in this town today, for sure."

Wrapped in chenille bathrobes—matching cover-ups for decent, stay-at-home girls—the Hearn sisters came downstairs to face their porridge.

Jennifer slumped into her chair, nursing the world's most lethal hangover—*pastis* on the rocks. Last night, she'd had the time of her life, tripping the light fantastic with sailors on the French ship. But now she was paying for it.

Her father was at the table, reading *The Daily News*. She glanced at the headline: "Inchworm Invasion!"

"Listen to this," said her father: "Whole city blanketed. Trees infested. Sidewalks slicked over with worm frass. Emergency rooms overwhelmed by 'slip-and-fall' fractures—broken wrists, twisted ankles, chipped tailbones..."

"Oooh how disgusting!" moaned Jennifer. "That makes me feel really ill."

"Straighten up and look smart" said Mr. Hearn, putting down the newspaper. "What a show you made of yourself on that French ship last night! This is going to get all over St. John's. You're a disgrace."

"Good morning, all!" sang older sister Theresa, taking her place at the table. An ex-nun, she'd been carried along by the new social upheavals of the mid-sixties, and had left her order. Now, fresh from the convent, she was settling back into life in the Hearn household.

"What's making you so chirpy?" groaned Jennifer. "And where did you end up last night? I had to convince you to tag along to the party with me and the girls from my French class, and the next thing I knew, you'd disappeared."

Jennifer munched on a piece of dry toast and continued. "You get away with everything and I get in trouble. Nothing ever changes around here. It's so unfair. I only went to the ship to practice my French. It'll come in handy if I ever get to go to Paris. That'll be the day!"

Back down on the wharf, there was activity: dockmen pulling dirty ropes, cranes squeaking, trucks backing up to loading docks. Flynn noticed a little Morris Minor, a gray Dinky toy of a car with the driving wheel on the wrong side, slowly making its way down the harbour drive. To his surprise, it came to a halt right in front of the French ship.

A gangly man stepped out, his long neck sticking out of a clerical collar. He adjusted his thick glasses and squinted at the ship.

I know who he is, thought Flynn. It's that Anglican minister with the English wife-from-hell. The two of them are not down on the wharf on a Sunday morning for naught.

The clergyman opened the passenger door and took his wife's hand; she stepped out—a stiff little woman, with salt and pepper hair set in even waves à la 1940s. As she strode past Flynn, he noticed her face. It was ashen.

Jesus Murphy, he said to himself, something's really up.

She marched over to the gangplank of the ship and confronted a perplexed guard.

Flynn cocked his ear.

"We must speak to the captain immediately. Our daughter has been missing since the reception on this ship last night."

With a nervous hand motion, the guard instructed her to wait where she was, then shouted up to the sentry on deck.

A few minutes later, the captain, puffy in the face, hurried down the gangplank, running his fingers through his thinning hair. With a weak smile and a nod, he introduced himself to the couple.

The minister's wife launched directly into a tirade, hitting High C from the outset. "My husband, the Reverend Moores, is minister at St. Luke's Anglican Church. We are shocked by what went on here last night. An absolute disgrace. Naval officers drinking with young girls barely out of school. And now it looks as if our daughter, Glenda, has been led astray by one of your men." She stopped to catch her breath, overwhelmed by her own indignation. "We have come here to tell you that the police have been informed that our daughter is missing, and we are holding you fully responsible."

At the mention of "police" the captain straightened into a military stance. "Yes, *Madame. Professeurs* and students from the university did attend our little *soirée*. But, of course, if there is a problem, we are 'appy to co-operate."

She shot him an icy stare, a specialty of hers. "At the very least, all your men must be questioned and the ship searched to see if Glenda is here." She looked up the gangplank, as if her slinky blonde daughter might appear amongst the sooty chimneys and military hardware on the deck. "The French Navy will have to answer to the police. My daughter should never have been pulled into a scandal like this. It's all very unfair." Then she turned and led her husband across the harbour drive to the car.

They drove off, skirting the edge of the curb, at a snail's pace.

"How could you be so stupid?" said Hearn to his wife. "To let those girls go to a 'French language practice' that was actually a party with sailors on a ship in the harbour?" He pushed his porridge bowl away. "Don't you know about the carousing that goes on at those events? I had to risk my reputation and go down there to bring the girls home out of it. And what was the first thing I saw after I managed to get myself on board ship? Our Jennifer, drunk and pushing a Frenchman around the dance floor, laughing and singing at the top of her lungs. Some 'French practice' that was! And that's not the worst of it. Then she went out and got sick all down the side of the ship. I had to make a public scene and drag her down the gangplank."

He glanced at Theresa. "And you're looking like the cat that swallowed the canary. What may I ask became of you last night?

I couldn't find you anywhere. Were you even on the ship? I thought you were my good daughter."

"All right *MomDad*," said Theresa, merging the two parents into a single entity like she always did. "Sorry I got in a little late. I was out walking with some people from the party, it was such a soft night."

Mr. Hearn drew his head back. "Well, that's lately come to you! Since when do you go walking just for the sake of it on a 'soft night?'"

The truth was, Theresa had just gotten home. But no one *knew that. Yet.* She ate her porridge, serene with her secret. The sweetest secret imaginable. "Treese," the plain little ex-nun and bride of Christ, *had been with a man.* Underneath the layers of robe and nightgown, she was transformed, still tingling from her night of "cultural exchange" on the ship with the French captain.

Naked, in his cramped quarters, a big white body with a ring of tan around his neck and two brown strips for forearms, he had shed respectful tears. "You're an untouched girl but so womanly, so wise, *une femme magnifique.*"

And she'd stretched out for him, pink-skinned and plump on the scratchy sheets of the narrow ship's bed. She knew in her own good judgment that her captain was sincere. And they'd made love, not with any frivolity but with serious intent.

Une femme magnifique, she repeated to herself now, with the deepest smile of her life.

Mr. Hearn banged his teacup on the saucer. "Treese, where's your head? Hurry up and get that food down ya. Can't you hear the bells ringing for Mass?"

She looked out the window at the Basilica tower, the belfry pigeons clapping their wings. I'm finished with playing the "holy daughter" in this house. Goodbye to all that!

The phone on the kitchen wall started ringing. Hearn jumped up to answer with a look of foreboding—it could only be bad news.

And it was.

Flynn was still surveying the scene at the French ship when the police arrived. Then, of course, he was immediately filled in by one of the young detectives.

"Some girl called Glenda Moores, a minister's daughter. It's a shockin' business. She's just been found dead. Her body was lying on the walking path by the Rennie's River. Apparently, she was down here dancing on the ship with them Frogs last night."

When he heard the girl's name, Flynn made the connection right away: That's Fred Duggan's little piece on the side. Duggie'd better have a good alibi for last night or he won't be pulling teeth in this town anymore.

Flynn's face remained impassive while he was given the details. Maybe if someone looked hard, they might have seen little electrical currents running through his green eyes, but, otherwise, his way of acting untouchable, like he owned everything, even the very ground you stood on, remained intact.

He put his arm around the detective's shoulders.

"That's an awful thing to happen to one of our local girls. Now you make sure you question those Frogs good and hard." He lowered his voice. "I figured these French parties would come to no good."

That done, he went straight back up the hill to his house. Hearing the clatter of his wife and daughter washing dishes in the kitchen, he snuck into his study, closed the door nice and tight and called Duggie.

"Jeez Dug b'y. You should keep your hands off young girls like that! If it comes out about you and her, there could be trouble. We can't have the police digging around our business, especially with the slum clearance not finished yet. It would be so unfair if that deal got stopped after all our hard work. So I'm going to keep a handle on the situation." He didn't wait for

Dug's response. "Let me know if they arrange an interview, and I'll be right over. What the hell happened to her anyway?"

"Beats me!" said Dug, winded, like someone had banged him in the chest, but trying to sound off-hand. "Last I saw of her, she was spittin' fire."

Last night, Dug had decided to break it off with Glenda. She was a hot little one, but she'd been getting too demanding. He stopped the car in the usual place, in the dark, under the red maples behind the ballpark.

"You're a great girl, but don't you think it's time you found a boyfriend your own age?" He patted her knee. "Sure, it can't be any fun for you, hangin' out with an old fella like me. You've got your whole life ahead of you!"

She jerked her knee away. "You've sure changed your tune—that's so unfair. You said you'd take me to Florida."

He turned the key in the ignition. "I've got to go home now, so you better get out of the car."

Tears shot into her eyes, but she pulled herself together. She flicked her mane of Twiggy-blond hair. "Lots of men would die to be with me. You creep, you can't—"

He leaned straight across her, grabbed the handle and pushed the car door open. "Oh yes I can! Now get out!"

Back at the breakfast table in the Hearn house, Jennifer was reacting to the shocking news: "Glenda Moores dead! How can that be? Sure, she left the ship early, never let any of those Frenchmen near her!" Colour raced back into Jennifer's hangover-white cheeks. "Holy Mary Mudder of God! This makes what I did look like nothing!"

Theresa's mind went straight to Jean-Marie, her gentle captain. This could mean big trouble for him. They were to meet in Victoria Park that night and she didn't want anything getting in the way. A big change was coming her way, and Treese was not one to hesitate once her mind was made up. In the convent, she'd been praised for her "leadership qualities" and singled out as "Mother Superior material." And this morning, she knew exactly what she was aiming for—a man. She'd already been looking up words in her French dictionary so she and Jean-Marie could really talk, make plans. *MomDad* were to know nothing for the time being. But now her tender night of love could all come spilling out like dirty water: "Sister Mary Perpetua," they'd say, "fresh out of the habit, had gone and lost her cherry to a French sailor."

Hearn had reached his boiling point. Ever since Mickey Flynn had rigged him a nomination to run for municipal councillor, he'd been, as his wife put it, "nothing but het up." Now, red-faced, his black hair slicked back with Brylcreem for Mass, blood drying around the shaving nick in his neck, he was a picture of despair.

"The police want to interview everyone who attended the do on the ship. I know this is a terrible tragedy, but the last thing I need is this kind of publicity—the police at our door right before the elections. It's so unfair." He sat down, his black eyes shining, and glared across the table at his wife. She pulled her robe around herself and folded her arms. She knew what was coming.

He started in.

"This is all your fault. You know how hard I worked to get this nomination. It's not everyone gets public support from Mickey Flynn. This makes a laughing stock of that blurb the election committee put out on me: *Respected member of the community, family man with two daughters.* I told you to keep a tight rein on the girls. This was no time to be changing the rules. You—"

The phone rang again. Hearn was about to burst. It was Mickey.

"The police told me they're going to your house. What in Jesus' name were you thinking, letting your girls run wild on that French ship?"

Glenda had left the French ship early to meet Duggie. He was waiting for her in his silver Cadillac, around the corner in the alleyway by Bowring's. A parking cop who'd seen the dentist pull up was only too happy to answer questions.

"He had the engine purring and the window down, his elbow hanging out. The radio was on and he was whistling along to the music. I remember, they were playing 'Harbour Lights.' Then the girl arrived, trotting fast up the alley steps in a shiny little frock, all peachy coloured, that new style—what is it they call it, mini-dress?"

"Oh! I thought to myself, Dr. Duggie's got a duckie on the go. I called out to her. 'Mind the inchworm-do now, darlin', sidewalks like a skatin' rink. Don't want to break your neck now!' But just as I said it, she slipped and went down. Tore her *stocking, scraped her hand and got a big greasy smudge of frass* on her dress. I went over to help her up. 'Poor thing,' I said, 'this is not your night. Why did you have to go and fall, eh? So unfair! Are you off to somewhere nice in your outfit?'"

'I'm fine and that's none of your business,' she snapped, mad and uppity, like it was my fault those worms drop out of trees. Sure, that's their nature! Anyway, she fussed for a minute, trying to wipe her dress but that only made it worse. Sad really. She looked upset and Dr. Duggie didn't even get out of the car. He was getting impatient."

"'Hurry up and get in,' he said through the open window. 'I haven't got all night.' She opened the car door. The light came on. I could see inside—all plushy red leather. Then she jumped in fast as a monkey and the car peeled off."

The dentist was interviewed in the breakfast nook of his executive house, one of the new oversized kind developers were building way in the back of town, on the berry hills.

He'd sent his wife and children off to Mass at the Basilica, the girl and boy dressed in matching blue-belted coats, like two little British royals. Mrs. Doctor Duggan, or "Buffy," as they called her, sat sullen amongst the worshippers. Duggie's playing around was going to be public knowledge now.

She'd heard Duggie come in last night, as usual—not too late, so he could get a good night's sleep, be fresh and handsome in the morning. He slipped in the back door and went straight to the little downstairs bathroom, where he washed himself.

Washing away his dirt, she'd thought. Then he came up the winding staircase to their pink, fluffy bedroom where she was pretending to sleep.

As planned, Flynn was at Dug's place for the police interview. He had his jacket off and sat at the table in a fresh white shirt and blue and red braces, looking relaxed, and, as ever, in charge. The two detectives had their notebooks out but were still waiting to begin their questioning—Flynn-the-kingpin was holding forth.

"I hear there was a lot of drinking on board that ship last night. You know, the b'ys down at the Port Authority were telling me—"

Jim O'Toole, the senior officer, cleared his throat loudly, cut Flynn off, and zeroed in on the dentist.

"It's a bit delicate, Dug b'y. It's true the girl was not underage, but just barely. And you appear to be the last person to see her alive."

Dug sat back in his captain's chair in the sunny window, light streaming in on the yellow wallpaper. He was all charm with his perfect white teeth and Florida-golf-course tan, but O'Toole could see he was nervous. He kept pulling at his cuff and brushing his lapel with his fingertips.

"I was done with her by midnight and home and in bed with the wife by 12.30," he said, as if Glenda were no personal concern of his. "The last I saw of her was when I dropped her off by the ballpark at the top of the Rennie's River trail. She'd normally run down the path to where it touches on her parents' backyard and sneak into the house through the basement door."

He looked O'Toole straight in the eye.

"But let's face it, Jim b'y. Girls like her can get up to all kinds of wickedness in the wee hours. Between you and me, she had a sadistic streak, could be a real tease… it takes a minister's daughter…"

He gave his lapel a brush, then added, clinically. "I'd say that girl had some kind of repression problem."

O'Toole scribbled a few notes, clicked his pen shut and put it down.

The junior detective, Tom Fudge, a clean-shaven Salvation Army boy, shuffled his papers.

"Nonetheless, Dr. Duggan, the fact still remains that you—"

With a loud scrape of his chair on the tiled floor, O'Toole stood up and motioned with his head to his sidekick that it was time to leave.

On the drive back into town, he ranted. "I know damn well what we're up against. Duggan's dentist practice is only the tip of the iceberg. He's a big man in the development racket, and I heard that Flynn, mayor or no mayor, is his silent partner— they made a fortune off that slum clearance. We're going to have to leave off on Duggan for the moment. Nothing ever changes around here."

"But that's not fair. We shouldn't go along with it. That poor girl is dead," said young Detective Fudge.

"I can tell you right now, my son," clipped O'Toole, "we got no say in this. If Mickey Flynn wants a cover-up, our line of questioning won't go nowhere."

Next stop was the Hearn house. Mister invited the two officers into the front room, where Theresa and Jennifer were waiting on the edge of their chairs, trying to look innocent. Each, in her own way, had just had the wildest night of her life. The officers kept their coats on and sat on Mrs. Hearn's brocade couch, legs spread, boots plonked on the floor.

O'Toole started the questioning. "Now then, Theresa. We know you left the ship very late and in the company of a man in uniform."

Mr. Hearn buried his face in his hands.

"We have testimony from a street bum who saw you come down the gangplank. The witness recognized you from your convent days—you'd served him Christmas dinner down at the mission. He saw you head up Carter's Hill arm in arm with a Frenchman, an 'ugly ole bugger' was how he put it—if you'll pardon my French. Where did you go? Was there any sign of young Glenda anywhere?"

Theresa cupped her hands in her lap, Mother Superior herself. "Absolutely not. That girl left the ship hours before everyone else."

O'Toole took a loud suck on his cigarette. "What do you know about this Glenda Moores? Is it true that she's fast and loose with the men?"

Jennifer jumped in. "Everyone knows about Glenda and men." She spilled out the gossip about Glenda, as if eager to redeem her own self: "Glenda was streets ahead of the rest of us girls. They say she's been going out with a rich dentist, way older than her, and she's even been two-timing him. She could be a real little bitch. Flirting with other girls' boyfriends. Men just couldn't resist her. I heard that—"

Jennifer stopped, took a big breath and sat back in the chair. "My God, I can't believe it. Glenda is *dead*!"

She continued talking, slowly now. "Glenda was in my French class. She was smart. And pretty. A beauty queen. She was just crowned Miss Freshette for 1966. She had her picture in the paper, sitting on her gold plastic throne... with that funny little false smile of hers." She paused again. "You know the real truth about Glenda? All the girls envied her for her good looks, but she had her troubles. Susan Miller told me that Glenda's mother is a cold witch. She found out what Glenda's been up to, and was planning to ship her over to relatives in some little village in England. Susan said Glenda's been a nervous wreck lately, doing crazy things. She was no angel, but it's so unfair what happened to her—only my age, and already *dead*."

But all the gossip in the world about Glenda and her wild ways had nothing to do with what really happened to her.

Young and attractive as she was, Duggie had grown tired of her. He'd filled her up with rum from his silver flask, had his way with her in the back seat, then tossed her off like a rag.

Half-drunk, she wobbled along the walking path in her satin pumps, her eyes clouded with tears. She knew he'd found someone else. Had seen him coming out of the Hotel with Dottie Handrigan, of all people, that red-headed bitch from the golf club. How can he even stand to look at her: dyed hair and all that makeup? I can do better than him anyway. I'm going to make a big change in my life and get out of here.

"*Just you wait till I start my pre-law at McGill!*" That's what she'd screamed at her mother in their very last argument. "You'll never get me to go to England. I'd die over there with those stuffy cousins."

Sitting on the couch in her wool suit, sipping tea from a china cup, the Reverend Mrs. Moores puffed out a tight little sigh of frustration. Another day of dealing with her unruly daughter. "You won't go to McGill or anywhere else without my permission, my lady... unless it's to hell for all your sins."

Glenda started snivelling. "I'm going to make something of myself. I'm going to be a lawyer, live in Montreal..."

But now, Glenda, the razor-sharp girl who went after what she wanted, the lonely, love-deprived mother's daughter—with all her hopes and dreams—was about to be no more.

At the turn in the pathway, by a dogberry tree with hundreds of worms hanging like grubby ornaments on the ends of their silken threads, all inching their fateful way down to the ground, Glenda slipped—good and hard this time. As she felt herself leaving the earth she called out.

No one heard her.

She flew into the midnight air, had her last glimpse of the summer moon and landed, cracking open the back of her skull on a big rock. Blood flowed out and pooled around her head.

Glenda was dead.

The next night, under the same summer moon, Jean-Marie, the gallant French captain, waited for Theresa inside the gate of Victoria Park, as promised. As she entered, she filled her eyes with him, and he beamed back at her. She was dressed plainly in a plastic rain hat and navy blue raglan, but he could see something sparkling on her collar—a rich red rhinestone cherry with a long sweeping stem. Removing his captain's hat, he kissed her tenderly, on each cheek. With the brush of his lips, she smelled the *Gauloise* cigarettes and *Eau Sauvage* cologne that would always be her Proustian memory of her first night of lovemaking, on a ship in St. John's harbour.

In the shelter of a gazebo at the back of the park, they found a nice clean bench, well away from slimy inchworms and nosy on-lookers. For hours, they sat and communed, talking and touching, eventually embracing, then kissing and kissing like lovesick teenagers.

"Will we have children, when you marry me and come live in my village in Arras?" he asked.

"Yes, we will," she said. "I will marry you and go live in your France and give you children. And nothing will stand in our way."

"Inchworm Inquest," said *The Daily News*. The police were pinning poor Glenda Moore's demise on the slippery conditions underfoot in all parts of the city. The questions stopped there. And investigators never did get to uncover all the dirty stories from the party on the French ship.

The following year, Jennifer Hearn made her long-awaited trip to Paris, where she managed to use a few choice words from her so-called French practice on the ship.

Glenda's mother kept an ashen face for the rest of her days. The daughter who had always been lost to her was gone for good.

As for Mickey Flynn and Duggie Duggan, there was no change in their luck—the two slum landlords aced it again. No scandal stuck to them. If Duggie carried a hard little grain of guilt about Glenda, nobody knew it. He took his wife on a swish cruise and bought her new jewellery. But not even all that wiped the sour look off her face.

Mayor Mickey made political hay of the inchworms, the danger they posed, and the tree-spraying campaign he would initiate to annihilate them, if re-elected.

And Hearn ran as a candidate on the "inchworm" ticket.

But as they say, *plus ça change, plus c'est la même chose*: prolific and resilient, the inchworms never did respond to spraying.

To this day, they return faithfully in season and dangle from the trees, arching and winking at you as if they own the place.

Starry Skies

Susan is sweeping the dock after last night's storm. She piles up the bits of twigs, the broken branches. The Dutchman in Spruce Cabin comes striding down the hill towards her. He's been doing that lately, turning up when she's working at her chores around the property.

"I saw you out in the field last night," she says, breaking a branch across her knee. She hesitates for a second, then adds, "I've never seen anyone do that, lie on the grass in the dark, looking up at the sky."

He smiles. "I haven't seen stars like that for years, not since my childhood in the little village back home."

Susan sees something in his eyes—softness, wonder. Afraid he'll notice her watching, she returns to her work, picks up another branch. But those luminescent blue eyes—she'd noticed them first thing when he checked in last week.

"What a peaceful place," he'd said as he signed the register. "You can hear the tiniest little birds peeping." A tall, slight man, all arms and legs, with a fuzz of blond hair on a balding scalp, he had a fatherly way about him. Protective. Susan had had an urge to put her head on his chest.

Now she goes back to her sweeping. The Dutchman looks out over the glistening blue lake. "Southern Ontario," he says with his Dutch accent and a tinge of fatigue. "What subtle beauty! I never knew. Not a grand landscape that knocks you over the head. Just natural prettiness. I've enjoyed my time here. It's been a real discovery. Your husband was telling me you have vacancies coming up. I'm eager to stay on for another week or two."

Something zings through Susan. A shiver. A thrill. What's happening to me? she thinks. A forty-year-old woman acting like a teenager, getting a crush on a stranger. And a client, to boot.

A flock of Canada geese flies overhead in a ragged skein, honking, flapping their wings, frantically changing places. Susan and the Dutchman look up. "They're so nervous," he chuckles, "trying to find their place in the V. Such precision. Must be stressful."

A country girl, nature sightings are no novelty to Susan, but she continues looking up. "I never thought of that. They are a bit frantic, aren't they?"

Greg comes roaring up to the dock on his red jet ski, shuts the engine off with authority and hops off, all muscle and smiles.

"Hello there, Piet," he says to the Dutchman. "If you want to go for a spin on this beauty, I can take you out in a few minutes. Just got to tell my wife the big news."

"Hey Susie, an insider on the council told Jack it looks like his marina expansion will get the green light."

Susan keeps sweeping, intently.

He turns to Piet. "Jack's our neighbour. This is a huge expansion. A hundred extra boats will bring new clients to our little business here." He glances at Susan and continues defiantly. "The wife's not entirely on board with the plan, but I think the bigger the marina, the better. We could expand too, build some new cabins..."

Susan whips around, branch in hand. "I told you I don't trust that Jack McAvan. He'll stop at nothing to make money. People come here for nature. Not big marinas."

Piet sits down quietly on the bench, crosses his legs and watches the wobbly line of geese heading for the horizon. Susan's at her branch pile, back turned.

Greg takes his cap off, runs his hand over his shaved head. "It's not going to be that big Susan, and you know very well if we are ever going to..." He stops, shaking his head at Piet, looking for male solidarity. But Piet has just caught sight of the muskrat steaming her way through the water with a mouthful of cattails.

Greg's big pecs tighten as he takes a shallow, frustrated breath. He puts his hat back on and runs up the steps to the house, two at a time.

Piet glances at Susan but she's turned her back again. There's just the sound of her cracking the branches, hard.

A few minutes later, Greg calls down to Susan. "You'd better get up here, the kids have got the living room turned upside down."

She takes off her work gloves and up she goes.

Another starry night. Susan sees Piet heading out to the field. She finishes the dinner dishes, then steps outside, making sure the screen door doesn't bang. Greg and the boys are in the basement watching baseball.

She walks slowly towards Piet, her feet heavy with hesitation. Dear God, I shouldn't be out here, she thinks.

Piet sits up when he sees the beam of her flashlight approaching.

"The sky is a feast for the eyes," he says, keeping his voice low, respectful. "Please, come join me. I was just looking at that big cluster. Over there, straight across from Orion's belt, you can distinguish Electra, one of the brightest stars in the sky."

Susan sits tentatively on the edge of the blanket. She looks up. "Yes, I recognize Electra. She's easy to spot. So luminous. Always shining and steady with that bluish light."

"If you don't mind me saying, I thought you might be a star gazer."

"I used to sit out and look at the stars when I was a kid, with my dad. We'd wrap ourselves in blankets on the dock."

"So this is where you grew up?"

"Yes, my dad built these cabins and ran the business. He loved this life, taking people out on the trails in the woods, portaging the canoe over to the little lakes nearby. There's quite a few of them, all unspoiled."

"What a lovely place to come from. It must be very dear to you."

He looks up at the sky. "How can you find words for it? Your mind just keeps travelling through the constellations. It's dripping with stars." He opens his arms, "Oh! It's so big, so grand."

Susan wants to be enveloped in those arms. She collects herself. "Oops," she says, slapping her hand, "Mosquitoes are out. Time to go in and put the kids to bed."

"Listen to this," says Greg, opening the morning mail. "Jack's marina expansion is on the council agenda next week. Says here, 'The public is invited to attend.'"

He throws the letter across the table. "I'm not going to that. I heard the cottagers on the lake have got a protest going, moaning and groaning about too much development."

"I'm surprised you don't want to turn up at the meeting to support your buddy McAvan," Susan says.

"I'm not going anywhere near those tree huggers. No way."

"Well, like it or not, you're married to a tree hugger," snaps Susan. She can hear the loathing in her own voice. She can't suppress it anymore.

Greg can hear it too, but he's determined to ignore it. "Come on now, Susie," he says with just a slight catch in his throat, "It's alright for those city folk in their precious cottages. You know damn well, none of the *real* locals are going for that environment thing. Back when your dad was running the cabins, a trickle of tourists was enough to live off. Those days are gone. Once Jack expands the marina, we'll be able to keep our cabins full with all those boaters. And I could take his new clients on fishing trips." Greg pushes his chair back from the table. "Get with it, girl. We've got kids to educate. And your dad would want us to do the right thing to keep the business going, wouldn't he?"

Susan picks up the council letter, waving it in the air. "Don't you associate my dad with schemes like this. McAvan wants to carve into the lake and build a gigantic high-tech installation. I'm sure Dad's turning in his grave."

Greg stands up, stifling his anger. In the old days, when they argued, he'd tease his young bride, running his fingers down her arm or kissing the nape of her neck. But that flirting is long gone.

Susan folds her arms across her chest, one of her many ways of keeping Greg out. In bed, she's become a fortress unto herself. For the past year, she and Greg have had the sad sleeping arrangement of a ruined marriage: she goes to bed early, he falls asleep on the couch, then comes in later, in the dark, and slides under the sheets, keeping to his side.

Now he gathers himself together, rolling up the sleeves of his work shirt. "Oh, come on Susie, you know very well that we have to develop if we're going to survive."

"How many times do I have to tell you, Greg? There's lots of ways to develop. All you have to do is take the trouble to read up on it. It doesn't have to be a mega marina."

"Fancy words, Susie. Next thing, you'll be hanging out with your new friends the cottagers, signing their petition."

Susan plops herself down at the computer, stares at the screen and says flatly: "I already have. I signed the petition last week."

"So that's where you've been lately. I wondered about those long shopping trips to town."

Greg grabs his cap and heads for the doorway. The two boys come running in past him. "Don't disturb your mom, now, boys," he says snidely. "She's joined the city folks, protesting against our own neighbours."

He turns to Susan, tightening the muscles around his eyes, "You'd better figure out which side your bread is buttered on."

The screen door bangs shut.

A windless morning. Blue sky, puffy clouds. Trees full of chirping birds. Greg's gone for the day with the kids, to visit their grandmother. Even Susan will admit that he's good with the boys. A devoted father, in his way. Teaches them to fish, hunt, play hockey, whip around the lake on the jet ski.

Susan's having a long swim across the silky lake, to the far point and back. That's where she does her thinking, and her ranting, these days. *It'll be so hard for the boys if their dad and I split. But I can't stand it anymore: Billy and John learning to drive that goddamn jet ski. Flooding the loon nests. Spilling oil in the lake.*

She finishes her swim, climbs out of the water, up the slimy dock steps.

Piet is there, reading a book on butterflies. "Come see these beauties," he says, showing her the book. "Swallowtails, aren't they gorgeous?" She picks up the towel and stands over his chair, water dripping from the tips of her shoulder length hair. "Oops, sorry," she says, brushing the drops off the book. A swallowtail swoops through the space between them, then pitches on Piet's hand, flittering its lacy-patterned wings. He watches it... then looks up in complicity at Susan.

She wraps the towel tightly around herself, almost ready to run, but steels her nerves. "Perfect summer morning," she says. "Not a breath of wind. Good day for a canoe ride. Would you like to do a portage over to Lake Nika after I finish cleaning the cabins?"

Susan has been dreaming of this, she and Piet paddling together. At first, she tried to wipe away the thought, but since she's joined the marina protest, hanging out with the cottagers at their wine and cheese meetings, she's turned some kind of corner.

"I've got my own truth," she'd said to herself, out swimming, that morning. She'd kicked her feet hard, fluttering the water, felt it flowing over her ankles. Greg's not going to snuff me out, make me comply. She'd headed for shore with a strong stroke. I'm going spend the day with that nice gentle Dutchman. And I'm going to turn up at that council meeting next week.

Susan and Piet are gliding across the lake, stroking in tandem. "You've got good technique, for a beginner," says Susan from the stern. She looks at his back. A different body type from her muscle-bound husband. A long spine, blond hairs on sinewy arms. She's been trying to guess how old he is. Sixty maybe? The canoe is a good place to start fishing for details. "When was the last time you were out on the water?" she queries, jay stroking expertly as they round the point.

"Oh, a good many years ago. When I was younger, in my forties, I did some sailing in the Waddenzee, back home."

"Solo sailing?"

"No, with my wife." He looks over his shoulder at her. "I'm a widower, you know. Lost my wife ten years ago."

So that explains the sadness, the sort of fatigue he has about him. He *lost* his wife.

They arrive at the portage point and begin carrying the canoe. "You're such a natural with all this," says Piet as they head along the path through the light-dappled woods. "I can feel how you really belong here."

"Oh, yes," says Susan. "This is my place in the world... such as it is."

Out of the woods, into a burst of sunlight and they're on Lake Nika. It's pristine. No cottages, no motorboats.

A heron stands dead still on a rock, intent on the hunt, his gray-blue reflection rippling on the water.

"He looks like a Japanese silk print," whispers Piet.

Susan whispers back: "This is my cathedral, where I come to worship. Only special people get to come here with me."

Piet touches her shoulder. "I'm honoured, Susan."

She feels a slight tremor in his hand.

They unpack the bags and spread out the picnic blanket. "Let's go for a little dip," says Susan. She's wearing her new red swimsuit under her shirt and shorts. It's not sporty like the suit she swims the lake in; this one shows her cleavage and shapely figure. She peels off her clothes and wades into the water, all curves and tanned limbs. Piet flops down on a grassy knoll. "You go ahead. I'll just relax."

She stays close to shore, treading water, moving her hands in quick motion. What am I doing? she thinks. I shouldn't have put on this sexy swimsuit. What must he think?

They picnic in the shade of a huge oak. Susan starts a Lake Nika game from her childhood: you have to listen for human-made sounds as hard as you can. They strain their ears but there's only the sound of bees buzzing, leaves rustling and the *plop* of a turtle falling off a rock into the water.

Piet starts in on his egg sandwich. "This is the life. It's so good to be retired."

Susan puts her shirt on, covering the cleavage. "You look too young to stop working," she says, trying not to sound flirtatious.

"Not as young as you think," says Piet, with that tinge of sadness. "My working days are over. But I liked my job. I ran a bicycle shop in Amsterdam."

Susan pours tea from a thermos, her dad's old thermos. She passes him a plastic cup. First when she and Greg were together, they'd picnicked on this very spot, drunk tea from these cups. The thought of Greg puts an edge to her words.

"I bet you've never done harm to anyone or anything, Piet."

"Oh, I wouldn't go as far as to say that. To tell you the truth," he looks sad again, "I sometimes worry that I harmed my wife."

"What do you mean, you harmed her?"

"By stopping loving her."

Susan flushes, embarrassed by the mention of "loving."

Piet keeps going. "I couldn't help it. I grew apart from her. We were never really on the same page. And then she got sick and died."

Susan rushes in: "Tell me about her." Then apologizes. "Sorry, I shouldn't stick my nose in like that."

Piet waves his hand. "It's no imposition. Sometimes it's good to talk to a stranger. No strings attached. Helps you get a clear picture of things."

Piet tells his tale: "Rebecca was an interior decorator. An accomplished woman. Always looking for change, the latest thing. I was attracted to that liveliness first when I met her. But then, with time, our differences came out. She wanted to get a new house, decorate with modern furniture. My little bicycle business wasn't enough for her. I was content in my shop, but she was always displeased with me—the way I dressed in my old wool sweater or spent weekends working the vegetable patch. It got to the point where all she did was criticize. We never had kids because she couldn't. So there was nothing left for us."

"She had her own truth, I guess," says Susan earnestly. "Your truth and hers just didn't match."

They sit in silence listening to the buzzing. Susan lies back on the picnic blanket and looks up into the oak branches. "This tree was hit by lightning years ago. See how scruffy and misshapen it is? I gave it a name when I was a little girl—Magdalena, after the Mary who got cured of her evilness. I always liked that story. The idea that even bad people can have their own goodness, their own truth."

Piet stretches out on his part of the blanket. "I like your scruffy tree." And then from somewhere inside it, a rich trilling whistle. "Oh look, it's an oriole. I can see his orange chest and his nest, hanging like a silk purse, from that high branch up there."

The oriole sings again.

"His note is true," says Piet, with a wry smile, "if it's truth you're after."

Again, the bird sings its pure, liquid song.

Susan sits up sharply, pours herself a fresh cup of tea, takes a gulp, then blurts out: "Here's what's true, Piet: I can't stand my husband anymore."

Piet sits up. "Oh dear, so sorry, Susan."

"It's like you said about you and your wife. Greg and I are just not on the same page. The romance dried up a long time ago."

Under the scruffy oak tree, Susan tells her story:

"I met Greg at the community college. He was taking car mechanics, and I was in landscaping. I knew from the beginning we had different ways of looking at things. It's the old cliché, opposites attract. I was young, and foolish enough to think the contrast was exciting. And Greg was so good looking and confident. We went out for a year, then got engaged. Greg liked the outdoors, wanted to settle down in the area and have kids. All the things I wanted. There was one problem, though: Greg and my father were like oil and water. Dad was quiet and soft spoken, the kind of man who looked after fallen baby birds. I'd seen how he acted around Greg—polite, because Greg was my choice—but his body language said everything. I remember once Greg came to visit in his motorboat and kept revving up the engine, smoking up the boat house. Dad scrunched his shoulders and closed his eyes a lot that day. He didn't like to disturb the peace and quiet of the birdwatchers staying in the cabins."

Piet listens, the fuzzy blond softness of him enveloping her.

"But I was stubborn, determined to do things my way. And Dad wasn't the type to interfere. Only once did he ever say anything. 'If your mother were alive, she'd be having words with you about marriage. You need to be able to share things with your spouse. Are you sure you and Greg can do that?'"

Susan gathers up the picnic dishes. "Dad died a few years after we got married. Then Greg left his job at the garage and came to run the cabins with me. But in his will, Dad made sure the business remains in my hands. Dad was right, of course. Greg's the wrong man for me. He's the kind of guy who thinks the lake is there for him to use, as hard as he can. He keeps saying how lucky we are to live in such a beautiful place, but he refuses to recognize that he's harming it. And, of course, he wants the boys to be like him."

A sombre look comes over her face. "But what I'm really torn up about is the kids. I should divorce Greg and be done with it. But I feel so guilty about leaving, breaking up the family. The boys are still so young, both under ten. I keep telling myself I have to stick it out for a few more years, 'till they grow up. But I don't think I can do it."

She stands up. "There, now I've really poured my heart out to a stranger. It does somehow make everything clearer." Her voice breaks, "…and it's not a pretty picture." She turns away, distressed. "The sun is leaving the lake. I think we'd better get going, Piet. Greg and the boys will be home, looking for their supper."

Lost for words, Piet scrambles to pack the knapsacks.

They carry the canoe back through the woods, in silence. Reloading for the last stretch of the trip on the big lake, Susan brushes against Piet's shoulder. She stops for a second, then throws her arms around his neck.

He holds her loosely. "We've shared a lot of secrets. Maybe too much. I guess we're two lost souls." He tries to comfort her, tapping her back awkwardly, then drops his arms. "Best we go home now. Your boys will be looking for you."

Embarrassed, Susan jumps back and gets on with pushing the canoe into the water. "Of course, Piet. Please don't mind me. I'm a mess these days. You're ever so kind to listen."

Getting into the canoe Piet slips in the mud and goes down hard. Susan runs to help. "I'm okay," he says grimacing and then smiles as she pulls him up. "You just steer us out of here, you're so good at that."

When they pull into the dock, Greg is sitting on the bench, ominous. "It's late," he says. "The kids and I have already eaten."

Susan fumbles with the rope as she ties up the canoe.

"Hi, Greg," says Piet, lifting himself stiffly onto the dock. "Susan was kind enough to give me a canoe lesson. My fault we got back late. I'm a slow paddler. Sorry." He heads up the steps to his cabin.

Susan hops out of the canoe. Greg undoes the knot she's just made. "I'm pulling the boat in, there's another storm tonight." He lifts the canoe out of the water in one fell swoop. Then he picks up the paddles and faces Susan. She can see the hurt in his eyes. "That's a bit much, isn't it?" he says. "You out there on a romantic ride to your favourite spot with that Dutchman? I can see from the mud on his clothes that you've been over to Nika. What were you up to? Rolling around on the ground together?"

"You've got it all wrong, Greg," says Susan over her shoulder as she escapes up the hill. "All wrong."

The debate over the marina expansion is heating up. Greg was right: most of the *real* locals are supporting McAvan's proposal.

Susan is volunteering at the church fair. Fran Driscoll, a widow who runs a camping site down the lake, has strong words for her while they fill the teacups: "I saw you in the supermarket having a cosy chat with that Ottawa woman who's heading up the protest against the new marina. I heard you've signed up. I'm surprised at you, Susan. Us locals should stick together. Poor Jack, he needs his neighbours' support. And to top it all off, Margot has up and left him, you know. Turns out she won't go along with the marina expansion."

At the news of the marriage breakup, Susan's heart skips a beat, but she answers smoothly. "Well, I can't blame his wife for bailing out. And I don't think what McAvan is proposing is very neighbourly at all. There's all kinds of evidence that his plan would seriously harm the lake and the habitats of endangered animals. The gray rat snake for one."

"We have a lot more to worry about than rat snakes," clips Fran, lining up the teacups. Then she zeroes in hard. "What's come over you, Susan? We have to make a livelihood from this lake. You have a family to think about. Poor Greg, he must be really upset with you."

Susan turns away, picks up the teapot and continues pouring. More guilt, she thinks. As if I didn't have enough. Then she rallies, puts the teapot down and turns back to Fran. "It's not poor Jack or poor Greg we need to worry about. It's the poor lake, can't you see that?"

It's late afternoon. Greg has gone over to the marina to help McAvan with a broken engine.

Tinkering with those bloody jet skis again, Susan fumes to herself. Besides the noise and the pollution, those machines are finicky, always breaking down. She glances down the hill and sees Piet coming in from his solo canoe ride. Bathed in the light of the low sun, he's melding with the scene, watching and listening, carefully balancing on the water. She goes down to the dock.

"Hello, Piet. Where have you been all week, I've hardly seen you."

"Oh, I thought I should, how do you say, *make myself scarce*. Don't want to cause trouble."

"Greg and I, we're in trouble alright, but it's not down to you."

They sit on the bench.

"It's been a rough week, Piet."

"Yes, I heard you and Greg arguing this morning as I passed by the kitchen window. That's a big divide between you, this marina protest."

"It feels like the end of something. It's scary—new territory for me, but there's no going back now. The public council meeting is next Monday. That's going to be a showdown. Greg's so mad that I'm going, he's taking the kids to his mother's. Doesn't even want to be home that day."

Piet puts a shaky hand on Susan's shoulder. "Would you like me to go to the meeting with you?"

Susan wells up with tears. "Yes, I would, very much." She pulls herself together. "Sorry about throwing myself at you last week at the portage. How embarrassing!"

Although she feels like doing it again.

A rainy night. Inside the packed council chamber, it's close and humid, windows steaming, umbrellas dripping. The protesters are buzzing with chat and determination, papers and statistics in hand. The councillors file into the room: three men looking like carbon copies of each other—white, balding and be-speckled, and two women—an older, wiry looking veteran politician in a navy-blue jacket and skirt and a younger, sporty looking woman wearing a golf shirt and pants.

The mayor files in last, a red-faced man, with the chain of office hanging over the bump of his belly. He calls the meeting to order. Councillors are invited to make individual comments on the marina proposal. The cottagers go still. Sitting in the front row with Piet, Susan scans the councillors' faces. Are they all corrupt? Do any of them care about the lake?

To Susan's surprise, each councillor finds fault with the proposal. The young councillor in the golf shirt speaks clearly to the point. "This proposal violates the zoning law, there is not enough shoreline on this property to permit further expansion."

Encouraged, the cottage protesters are muttering and shuffling in their chairs.

The last councillor to speak is the wiry veteran politician: "We should remember, however, that interpretation of the zoning laws can be very fluid." She points her birdlike face at the young golf-shirted councillor. "Other precedent setting cases should be taken into consideration."

The mayor keeps a deadpan face and invites the public to make comments. A long line-up forms at the microphone. The speakers are a mixed bag: cottage-owning lawyers from Toronto who have researched their environmental case, American cottagers who want to protect their property but are not used to Canadian ways, and even a few *real* locals who simply can't stand Jack McAvan and his greed. As the protestors, one after another, plead for protection of the tranquility and the natural environment of the lake, the level of outrage rises. "This proposal is a disgrace," shouts out a watery-eyed elderly man from his seat. "You should be ashamed of yourself."

McAvan stands up and heads for the mike. His eyes dart around as he makes a case for himself. Keeping his voice low, he declares humbly how hard it is to run a business like his.

"Now he's the victim," whispers Susan to Piet. "Look at the wounded look on his face."

"I'm a good neighbour," McAvan continues. "I let people hike on my land, swim at my beach." He finishes off with a few staccato pleas. "I bring a lot of business to the area. I think my neighbours should think about giving back to me. I can't survive without this expansion."

The mayor clears his throat then speaks in a slow drone. "It seems to me that there is a lot at stake here. I am therefore going to move that the proposal be sent to our lawyers for perusal."

Despite murmurs of outrage from the cottagers, the mayor's motion to defer the vote passes. Four of the councillors who had raised the issue of shoreline length go along with the mayor's ploy to keep the proposal alive. Only the golf-shirted woman votes against it.

Piet and Susan are driving down the dark country road to home. Susan throws her bundle of protest papers into the back seat. "It's all over. We've lost. The mayor and his cronies are bound to have their way."

"Maybe they'll only approve part of the expansion. You can't lose hope."

"I know what we're dealing with here. The developers always win out." Susan rolls down the window to the night air and the chirping of crickets. "Everything's definitely over, Piet..." She looks across at him, choking up. "My marriage included."

Piet stops the car by the lake. "Let's get out for a few minutes and look at the sky."

They stand under the canopy of stars.

"There's Electra again," says Piet. "You can always find her up there, shining away. It's a comfort."

Susan looks at the star then turns to Piet. "You'll never know what a comfort you've been to me. I wish you didn't have to leave tomorrow." Again, she wants to put her head on his chest.

He takes her hand with his two hands. "I've developed a real fondness for you, Susan… and I'll be sorry to say goodbye in the morning but it's time for me to get back home."

He gently removes his hands. "You know, I think you'll be fine. You're a good mother and you're determined and capable, like our Electra, always shining and dependable. There's no need for you to feel guilty. You and Greg can work something out, even if it means divorce."

A shiver of dread runs through Susan. "It's hard to keep shining. But for the kid's sake, I'll have to."

She opens the car door. "We'd better get back. Greg left a message that he and the boys will be home tonight, after all."

When they get to the house, Susan sees the dark hulk of Greg's truck parked in the driveway. She gives Piet a peck on the cheek and jumps out of the car.

Her voice trails off as she heads for the house. "Thank you for everything, Piet. Good night, good night."

She goes inside. Greg's watching TV but doesn't turn to greet her.

Next morning, ruffled and sleep-deprived, Susan checks Piet out of his cabin. Then she goes out on the hill to say goodbye to him.

Before getting into his car, he takes her in his arms. "You'll be fine," he whispers into her ear. "I know you'll find a way."

And then he's gone.

Susan smells a whiff of gas. She turns towards the lake. Down at the dock, Greg is helping the boys rev up their new, kid-sized jet-skis.

A Big Opportunity

Everything started when the local tourist lodge hired my husband as a fishing guide for a new "high profile" guest. On the first trip out on the lake, my son Brendan went along to give his father a hand.

"I don't care how wealthy and important he is, Dad, I don't want to go fishing with that Malloy fellow anymore," Brendan said when they came home that night. "He's so full of himself. Just wants to drag as many bass as he can out of the water."

My ears perked up. It was unusual for Brendan to take a strong stand on anything, especially with his father.

"Don't condemn Mr. Malloy outright," Owen said. "He's a bit of a talker but he seems okay. You meet all kinds, and with tourism being slow, we can't pick and choose clients. But if you find him that offensive, Bren, it's best you take a break and get on with your university work."

After a week of fishing with Malloy, Owen came home with his pockets full of money. And he was all pepped up, excitement in his eyes, like he'd been out having a good time with an old friend.

"A couple more trips with Mr. Malloy and we'll have enough to replace the old kitchen stove," he said with a real chortle. "And he wants to keep fishing all summer. If I get a few other clients, our money problems could be a thing of the past by the fall, Mavis. This is a real stroke of good luck!"

I remember looking at the pile of bills on the kitchen table. "That Malloy sure is generous with his tips. I wonder where he gets all the money." I can't help being the suspicious type. My mother before me was like that—never let my dad step off the straight and narrow, even if it meant doing without.

"Desmond Malloy's a well-known businessman and he's high up in Ottawa, close to the prime minister," said Owen, looking puffed up, like he was suddenly close to the big man himself.

The name Desmond Malloy rang a bell. It seemed to me I'd seen him mentioned recently in the newspaper, in an article on lobbying in Ottawa. We have a little library here in Balla-on-the-Lake, so the next day, I went over there and looked through the backlog of papers until I found the piece in question. My suspicions were confirmed. Sure enough, Malloy was some kind of "backroom organizer" and "associate" to the PM, who had appointed him to several important boards. The journalist referred to him as a "master wheeler-dealer" in the "cut and thrust" of the Ottawa scene in the 1980s.

"You mind yourself with Malloy," I warned Owen, smelling a rat. "He's involved in shady deals, by the look of it."

"Oh, don't worry, he's strictly above board," proclaimed Owen, holding up his hand like a preacher. "He told me himself, those allegations never amount to anything. It's all politics. When you get close to the PM, the press tries to bring you down."

I could tell he was mouthing Malloy's words. "Are you sure you're not taken in by his talk?" I asked as gently as I could. "An experienced operator like him would be slick when it comes to covering his tracks."

"Don't be like that." Owen sounded almost hurt. "He's the finest kind. You should hear about the charity work he sponsors. He does a lot of good in the world."

"I wonder what else he does in the world," I said, unable to stop myself.

Owen surprised me with his strong reaction. "Now Mavis, I know you come from a long line of high and mighty women, but sometimes you need to tone your judgement down and give people a chance." He left the room in a huff.

I hated it when we quarrelled, when the fault line in our otherwise smooth marriage cracked open. But sometimes my strong opinions clashed with Owen's easy-going nature.

And it seemed he'd taken quite a shine to Desmond Malloy, so I'd have to bite my tongue on the subject.

Before long "Des" and Owen were on a first name basis and Des had become a household word around our place. Owen quickly earned enough guiding him to buy the new stove. But even though it was the latest model with a special warming oven, I always felt uneasy about using it. My mother's warnings about "ill-gotten gains" kept running through my head.

Des had a big showy motorboat with a fancy name written on the side, "Power Glide." You could hear the roar of the engine all over the village when he started it up, and it left a permanent oil slick on the water by the dock. The boat was equipped with fish finding sonar. Owen normally used a rowboat with a small motor when sussing out the bass in the shallow reeds or out in the deep fishing holes of the lake he knew so well.

"With all that equipment, you'd wonder why Des needs you to guide him," I remarked to Owen. Clearly, I was not doing a good job of curbing my tongue.

Owen flinched but defended Des. "Oh, he likes to play with the sonar," he said, laughing, "but he's willing to learn about the bass and what complicated little creatures they are. No fish finder could ever tell you their likes and dislikes, how their moods are connected to the temperature of the water or the phase of the moon."

That was the beautiful thing about my husband—his respect for the lake and knowledge of the fish. He put his hand on my shoulder to reassure me: "Des knows that."

But Owen did enjoy going out in that snazzy boat with Des. They'd whizz out the channel from the village dock, the steel trim glinting in the sun and both men with the biggest kinds of smiles on their faces.

Brendan used his break from guiding to finish his poetry project for the distance creative writing course he was taking at Ottawa U. I was happy to see Owen supporting Bren's writing. We didn't always have the same ideas about our son's future. I was hoping Bren would go on to teachers' college when he finished his BA. I did enjoy having a son who majored in English and wrote poetry. But Owen worried about him being "too much of a romantic" with his "poetry" because "there's no certain future in that."

This made me smile to myself, as most of Bren's poems were about uncertainty: neat little verses about truth and the impossibility of understanding the universe. There was one line that went: *How do you know what's true when everything comes hurtling at you?*

Eventually, Mr. Malloy decided to invite friends from Ottawa to join him on the fishing trips, so Owen needed Bren's help. To my surprise, within a few days of guiding with the famous Des, Bren was coming home with the same lift in his step as his father, a kind of titillation at being in the company of the big honcho from Ottawa. Again, playing the devil's advocate, I commented to Brendan that he seemed to have had a sudden change of heart regarding Mr. Malloy.

His response was downright defensive. "I was wrong about Des before. It turns out he's a real statesman, works for the government on international trade committees. I'm learning a lot from him."

First Owen and now Brendan, I thought. Malloy's got hold of the two of them. Hook, line, and sinker.

It wasn't long before the whole of Balla was buzzing with Des Malloy gossip. Our village is only two hours from Ottawa, and someone always knew someone who was cousin to this one or that one who worked in the capital, so information came down the line: Des was a divorced man and had one child, a daughter who lived with the estranged wife—very estranged, they said. I also heard the word "womanizer" several times, and rumours circulated about young secretaries being lured by Des to drink champagne in expensive hotel rooms.

Owen came home on the Friday of the Canada Day weekend with something on his mind. I could tell just by the tilt of his head. He spoke cautiously, "Well, Mavis, I know you're leery of Des, but he has no relatives here, and he's a hell of a nice fellow so I was thinking we should invite him to the barbecue on Monday."

Des turned up at the barbecue with a case of beer, looking very dapper. I'd seen him from a distance down on the dock with Owen, but this was my first good look at him. He was a tall, broad-shouldered man with a big head of thick blond hair, cut in a fancy way to show off the waves. He was wearing a nicely-pressed summer shirt with a Canadian flag pin on the collar, white pants and shiny white loafers—the kind of outfit you see men dressed in on the cover of golf magazines. On the whole, he was a handsome sort, but his good looks were marred by a slightly off-centre nose.

The beers flew out of the case. Owen was under doctor's orders to avoid alcohol because of his heart condition, but I saw him gladly accepting a Molson from his new-found friend. Des was all smiles with his even white teeth, and he was full of chat, at ease, like one of the family. Before long, my young nephews and nieces were standing around him in a circle, drinking and laughing at his jokes.

"I'm proud of my Irish Ottawa Valley roots," he said, raising his glass, "And of course, your ancestors here in Balla came from the Emerald Isle. Here's to the Irish!"

He's not my Irish, I thought. I'm not part of his clan.

Later on, my sister's daughter, Maude, who was twenty-one, working in Ottawa and thought herself quite the young sophisticate, ended up at the bottom of the garden in a long *tête-à-tête* with Des. I noticed that he kept putting his hand on her back and leaning in close to listen to her.

I was watching all this from my perch at the picnic table. With my arthritis and swollen knees, I'm not one for standing around with a drink in my hand. Eventually, he made his way over to me and sat down. That's when I noticed the fancy cologne he'd doused himself in. "You have a beautiful family," he said, clasping my hand, uninvited. "I was close to my mom and dad, you know. They're both gone now but I have my daughter, Hanna. I've just bought a cottage here in Balla, and I'm hoping to get her out here fishing this summer. She's a lovely girl and I'll bring her over to meet you."

I gave him a half-smile and nodded. That seemed a bit forward to me, inviting himself over with his daughter. And on top of that, his voice was oily. Everything he said sounded slick. With the pushy way he was barging into my family, I drew back. But he either didn't notice or didn't care. The next thing I knew, he started in on Brendan, getting all emotional about what a "bright young man" Bren was and how I must be "very proud" because he definitely had the brains to "make something big of himself."

That night when we were cleaning up, I told Owen that it seemed strange to me that someone as important as Des Molloy should be so interested in hanging around with the likes of us.

"Oh, he's not that fancy," said Owen. "He's a simple guy with a big heart. And you know something, I think he's lonely."

After that, Owen started bringing Des around to the house for supper. The men would sit outside with a beer while I puttered around the kitchen. It was extra work for me—because of all the money Des was giving us, I felt obliged to put out the Sunday dishes and set the condiments in little bowls. That's the problem with accepting generosity: there's always that niggling feeling that you should feel grateful.

Through the open kitchen window, I'd hear Des's greasy voice, regaling Owen about his adventures fishing in the Caribbean with the PM or hunting at a private lodge in Labrador. Owen would listen, wondrous. He'd never done anything grand like that. Hardly ever been out of Balla, for that matter.

Over supper, Des usually did most of the talking. I'd get through the meal, keeping my thoughts to myself. He was all superlatives. That man could pin a hyperbole on anything: his friend was "the best guy on earth," his car was "a dream on wheels," his work in Ottawa was "top-notch development for the country" and even our humble little Balla was the "prettiest little village in Ontario."

As summer wore on and the visits from Des multiplied, I grew impatient with keeping quiet. "You're devoting all your guiding time to Des. Does the lodge go along with that? It's starting to feel like we're bought and paid for by him," I blurted out to Owen as he put on his pyjamas one night after a supper with Des.

Owen was indignant. "That's not true, Mavis. I'll still be accepting new clients from the lodge, and I work hard for the money Des pays me."

But I continued speaking my mind. "And another thing, doesn't it seem childish to you that a man of Des's standing should need to prop himself up with big talk, cover himself in glitter and gilt?"

"It's not glitter and gilt," snapped Owen. "It's just that he likes to think positive. And he has high standards." He shook his head. "Why don't you admit it, Mavis. You've developed some kind of grudge against this man. It's written all over your face at the dinner table. It's unfair you know."

I stood my ground. "I know vanity when I see it, Owen."

Owen got into bed, switched off the light and turned his back to me. "As far as I can see, the only vanity here is you and your high opinions."

This was a rare event for us—going to sleep in anger. We had a loving marriage with lots of happy memories, right back to when we were a young couple and I helped out with the guiding, before my arthritis set in.

Now I lay awake fretting over the divide Des was creating between us.

Should I try somehow to develop a liking for this man? Could I be wrong about Des?

When I think back on it, that was a summer like no other—our family at Des's beck and call, money flowing, me sitting on my anger. Owen was feeling chipper, but I worried he might be overdoing it, given his heart condition. And I noticed that he was often ruddy-faced. He dismissed my concern. "Oh, that's just from being outdoors, living the good life."

And then there was my Brendan. I was always protective of him. He was an impressionable boy and on the sensitive side. As a child, he'd had a slight stutter, but he'd more or less overcome that through sheer determination. Nonetheless, when he was stressed or excited, the stammering would come back.

"Des knows all the ins and outs of...pa...pa...PARLIAMENT," he bragged to me one night after yet another supper with Des. I knew that chatting with the likes of Des was a stretch for Bren. He'd never been the sociable sort, but here he was, taking life lessons from the smooth-talking Mr. Malloy.

By mid-summer, Des had moved into his "cottage," the old doctor's residence that he'd bought and was renovating. He was even installing a massive floor-to-ceiling fireplace in the living room. Very grand for Balla. There was no end of gossip about the lavish additions to Doc Smith's old house. When the fireplace was completed, Des decided he wasn't satisfied with the workmanship and demanded the whole thing be torn down and rebuilt. The workers were disgruntled, to say the least. The place was three times as big as our little stone cottage with its low ceilings and slanting floors. It was like another world—a real "bachelor pad," people said, with men from Ottawa turning up there in smart cars, often with women in tow.

But despite the comings and goings, Des remained the lone true resident of his summer palace. There was no sign of his long-lost daughter, Hanna.

Owen, on the other hand, was over there a lot. It was no sense my objecting. "I'm just helping Des finish the place off," he'd say. But he was also helping Des with the odd libation, I suspected.

One night he came home a little drunk and noticeably short of breath. I was concerned. "You can't keep up this pace, Owen, over at Des's all the time. It's too much for your heart."

"Now Mavis," he replied, his cheeks on fire, "Don't trot out your dislike for Des. He's become a good friend."

I raised my voice. "You're overdoing it, Owen." Then I went ahead and took a huge stab at Des. "I don't think Des Malloy cares about your well-being. He's too tied up with his own glory."

Owen banged his toolbox down on the kitchen table. "You truly are your mother's daughter, Mavis. When are you going to cut out the moralizing?"

The next morning, I apologized for going over the top. Owen admitted he was feeling a little strained and vowed he'd slow down. Then he started sending Brendan over to help Des out. As the days went by, Bren's visits got longer and longer.

"Des and I were chatting," he said one night when he came home late for supper.

His father was more than pleased. "That's good, Bren. Des can give you some pointers. He's your man."

Then it happened. On a stifling hot Tuesday morning, when I was in the garden hanging out the clothes, Bren appeared out of nowhere at the fence. He was crying. "Come quick, Mom!" he called. "Dad's been taken to hospital. He was helping Des lift the new motor out of the truck and collapsed."

When I got to the hospital, I found my Owen, my big-hearted, steady, loving husband, the gentlest man in the world, laid out on a stretcher—eyes closed, dead and gone.

Bren and I were left to mourn in our little stone cottage. For the rest of the summer, Owen's fishing cap hung on the hook by the door. Neither of us had the heart to remove it. Everything felt grisly and hopeless. Bren was lost, a fatherless boy at twenty. He kept spinning around the house, trying to do his father's chores. And I was the opposite, so sad my limbs had gone heavy. I could barely get off the chair. For Bren's sake, I tried to keep going, but it was a hard row.

Des came around to the house several times after the funeral. It's all a haze in my memory, but he did seem genuinely torn up about Owen. I was furious with Des for letting my vulnerable husband lift a heavy engine, but I had to acknowledge that Owen had been truly fond of him: strange bedfellows as they were, they'd been good friends.

"Owen was a gentleman," said Des, his eyes glistening. "You and Owen are the finest kind of people and this son of yours is a credit to you both."

The next thing I knew, desperate for diversion, Brendan went back to guiding on the "Power Glide" with Des. Still grieving, and without strength to object, I succumbed to the idea that being out on the lake helped the boy feel close to his dad. So despite Owen's passing, "Des" remained a household word around our place.

"Why don't you spend time with your own family? Your uncles and cousins?" I said weakly, as Bren headed out the door one morning to meet Des.

"But Mom, Des is showing me how trade deals work." He paused in the doorway. "There's a big world out there beyond teachers' college," he stated with a sort of forced certainty. "Des says I'm cut out for the law."

I was caught short. "The law?"

"Des thinks I can stay on at Ottawa U and go into the law school next year, no problem."

"We'll see," I said, with a drag in my voice. "That could be a long and expensive road. And what about your dream to be a teacher and a writer?"

Bren shrugged his shoulders. "Mom, Des says if I go into Law, he'll pa... pa... PAY for the whole shot. And not only that, he'll arrange for me to work for him as a part-time assistant. It's a big opportunity."

"Your father and I never took handouts," I sputtered. "It's better to do things under your own steam."

Bren answered with a coolness and distance I'd never felt from him before. "I know it's what Dad would have wanted. It's a big opportunity. And I'm going to take it."

I was stunned by the finality in Bren's voice. Suddenly, I no longer had a say in his future. My lovely boy, trying to be a man.

Shortly after, I received a letter from Des, announcing that he would pay for Bren to attend Ottawa U Faculty of Law. It was a done deal.

With no real say in anything, all I could do was try to set my fears aside. Bren was a clever boy and I had to trust that he'd find his way.

The next year, Bren entered law school and, as promised, became Des Molloy's part-time assistant. It was deathly lonely for me back in Balla. Eventually, he found time to come home for a flying weekend.

The second he came in the door, I could see that he was transformed. "I hardly know you with that spiffy haircut and those tailored clothes," I exclaimed. He looked like a stranger, a mini-Des, right down to the whiff of expensive cologne.

Bren was delighted with himself. "I go to all kinds of high-end places with Des, even to meetings 'on the Hill,' so I have to dress for the role." As he gushed on about his new life, I noticed that his language was laced with Des-like hyperbole—the "top-level" negotiations he attended, the "super-sharp" minds he encountered.

Where was my Bren who wrote poems about uncertainty and looking for truth? "Don't lose yourself around all that power," I warned as I served him up a piece of his favorite apple pie.

Bren replied with a coolness that hurt me to the quick. "It's not at all what you think. You have no idea about the Ottawa scene, Mom. But how could you, living in Balla all your life?"

Thanksgiving was approaching. "Looks like I won't be home for the holiday," said Bren on the phone. I could hear guilt in his voice. "Des has an important meeting at his place in the Bahamas and I'm going along for the experience. It's a big opportunity."

At Thanksgiving, I received a huge floral arrangement that just barely fit through the front door. It sat on the table all weekend looking ostentatious and out of place.

Come June, his exams over, Bren came back to stay in his old room in our house. But he spent most of his time at Des's place, hobnobbing with those Ottawa "international trade" men. It was an exciting existence for a summer job in Balla. But I knew my Bren, and I could see that the initial thrill of the job, the clarity in his eyes, the flush in his cheeks, had worn off and been replaced by something more sober. Now, more often than not, he seemed preoccupied, if not nervous, staring into space, flipping through his notes.

It was going on for midnight. I was just heading to bed when the phone rang. Normally, Bren answered but that time, I got to it first.

"Oh, good evening, Mavis." It was Des. Right away, I knew he was drunk.

"How are you tonight, my fine woman?" he slurred. I frowned, and before I could respond, Bren grabbed the receiver.

He listened to Des's instructions with a grave look, then jumped into action. The screen door banged, and I thought to myself: What could he be up to at this late hour?

In the middle of the night, I was awakened by the thud of a car door closing. I looked out the window and saw Bren, unloading boxes from the back of Owen's old truck. Then I heard his heavy tread as lugged them upstairs and stacked them in our little attic.

I dragged myself out of bed and confronted him on the landing, losing all control. "What are you up to? Moving boxes around in the middle of the night? And why didn't you ask my permission to put files belonging to Des Malloy in our attic? God knows what's in those boxes!"

"Why do you have to be so suspicious of Des?" Bren shouted. "There's nothing wrong with these files. It's just business."

"I'm worried you're in over your head, Bren."

Bren's shoulders were twitching. "You're overreacting, Mom. Let me do my job."

I went back to bed with the thought that there was no getting through to Brendan. I'd lost him as surely as I'd lost Owen.

August marked the end of a year-long fundraising campaign to restore the Balla community hall. I was on the Restoration Committee and attended the meeting where the Chair read out a letter from Des Malloy, offering a huge contribution that would allow the work to be completed on time.

Now he's becoming the village saviour, I thought.

On the Saturday of Labour Day weekend, there was a roast beef dinner and dance to celebrate the newly renovated hall. Des attended, of course, along with his slick sidekick, businessman Jean Leroux, who had also thrown some money in, and a cohort of Ottawa friends, both women and men, mostly young, especially the women. At the dinner, the Chair paid tribute to Des. He was at his jovial best and made a speech about Balla and how proud he was to be a property owner in our historic village. There were admiring smiles all around the hall. Everyone was impressed by his generosity. I kept looking at his glowing face—he did seem sincere about the giving. It's so complicated, I thought, this prancing around in the world of money. You get to take but you also get to give and feel good about it.

After dinner, the tables were cleared for the dancing. Des had once again got hold of my young niece Maude, much to my sister Mabel's dismay. "Look at that devil, he's determined to have Maude and she's in way over her head. He's too slick for our Maudie and he's old—never mind that swishy hairdo, it's all *designed to hide the bald patch on the top of his head.*"

Old or not, Des was swirling our Maudie around the dance floor in her purple chiffon dress. He was all energy and smooth control. "Dear God, he gives me the shivers," said Mabel.

But the big surprise that night was to see my Brendan dancing. His chosen partner—or had he been chosen?—was a slim young woman with short, spiky black hair and an unsmiling face. She and Bren were stuck together like glue, just barely moving their feet. I'd sensed for some time that he had a girl in his life, had heard him muttering on the phone in the hallway. So here she was.

During the pause, he brought her over to meet me. "Mom, this is Lauren, from Montreal. She was in my constitutional law class."

Lauren was sort of pretty with a slightly too long jaw. She cracked a brief smile in her sombre face. I was glad to see that she was a modest-looking girl, simply dressed, not dripping with glitter like the young women in Des's group. Maybe Bren hadn't lost his values, after all. What kind of law are you interested in?" I asked, interviewing her.

She grabbed Bren by the arm in a proprietorial way. "I'm not sure yet, but Bren and I hope to open an office together one day."

Bren and I. She's got plans, I thought.

It was a cool September morning, with the leaves turning and a lop on the lake. I put on my fall coat and took my usual stroll to the marina shop to get the *Toronto Star*. I picked up the paper, and there was the headline, large as life in black capital letters:

DESMOND MOLLOY CHARGED WITH INFLUENCE PEDDLING

Paralysed, I stood staring at the wall, for how long, I don't know. The girl behind the counter kept asking me if I was alright—she sounded miles away. I wobbled home, clutching the newspaper to my chest, hiding the headline.

When I got into the house, I sat at the kitchen table with my coat on and read the details of the case: the RCMP were charging Des for using his influence to ensure that an arms manufacturing company called "Defence Options" was issued the export permit for an arms shipment to Saudi Arabia. Des had allegedly received a kick back for the favour. The CEO of the arms company was one Jean Leroux. I went back in my mind to Leroux, whom I'd seen at the charity dance, his dark eyes and gold chain resting on chest hairs sticking out of his open collar.

I put the paper down, my hands shaking. What would happen to Bren now? Would he lose his job? Would this be the end of Des's support for law school? At the same time, a fury was rising in me: How dare Malloy bring my innocent boy into this corrupt world! I thought of Owen—how shocked and disappointed he would have been, how it would have torn his heart out to see our Bren drawn into such ugliness.

The poor boy must be shaken up, I thought. When I called him, he didn't answer until after quite a few rings. "Hi Mom." I could feel how tight his throat was.

"I've seen the headlines, Brendan. These are serious accusations. Tell me the truth, will you be implicated in this scandal?"

"Not directly," he said, in the first of many hedges on the subject. "It's complicated."

It wasn't, of course, at all complicated. As Des's assistant, Brendan had been party to much of what had gone on.

After weeks of speculation and endless stories about Des and his cronies in the papers, a court date was announced. My worst fears were confirmed: Bren would have to testify. During the lead-up to the trial, he stayed mostly in Ottawa, being coached by Des. Then he turned up in Balla one night in November. We'd had some freezing rain and he slipped on the walkway, banging his head on the step, and appeared at the door with a bleeding cut over his right eyebrow. What a sorry sight he was. Weight had dropped off his already slim frame and his shoulders slumped in defeat.

Over supper, he began to talk it out. It was all so sad, but I felt I had my old Bren back.

"I never understood what was happening, Mom, I swear to God. I thought Des was above board. But it's difficult to keep track of how men like him operate—there are holding companies and trusts and layers and layers of ways of hiding what you're doing." He gave a little shudder.

"But what he's asking me to say in court amounts to straight-out lying. How can I face the court with all the 'maybes' and 'not sures' and 'can't remembers' Des wants me to use? And anyway, if someone with a sharp eye takes a good look at the documents in those boxes we stored in the attic upstairs, they'll discover what Des and Jean Leroux were up to."

Bren and I sat up in our little kitchen next to Des's fancy stove with its shiny buttons, talking and talking, trying to find a way out. It felt like sticky corruption had dripped all over us. In the wee hours of the morning, Bren finally came to the conclusion that he'd have to tell the truth and turn the boxes in as evidence.

Bren was crying now. The striving to fit into Des's world was over. "I don't know what will happen to Des if I testify against him. He's done so much for me, Mom, and I'm grateful. But there's no other way out, as far as I can see."

I climbed the stairs to bed with lead in my feet.

The trial finally got going in March. On the day that Bren was called to testify, my brother-in-law drove me and my sister to Ottawa. We got there early, walked through a crush of reporters to get into the courtroom, then sat on a hard bench, waiting for the judge to enter. Mabel was eager to see the demise of Des Malloy. Her Maudie had fallen hard for him and his champagne existence, only to be tossed aside when summer came to an end. "These people think they can play by their own rules," said Mabel, fidgeting with her purse.

Jean Leroux appeared first, looking like everyone's trite version of a rich villain: sporting a Caribbean tan and decked out in an expensive blazer with brass buttons. His answers were glib and slippery, "I engage in hundreds of transactions yearly... have no recollection... Des Molloy is a good friend and a fine Canadian..." He ended with a defiant sweep of his hand, as if the charges only amounted to a joke.

Then Bren was called up. In contrast to the flamboyant Leroux, he looked haggard and shrunken. Des's lawyer, a tall skinny man with his pant legs flapping, came at Bren with scalpel-sharp questioning. He kept trying to catch him out on his memory of dates and times. Bren strained to answer honestly but got more and more confused as the lawyer upped the pressure. "Why would you have stashed those papers in your house in Balla? For your own personal gain?"

Bren got indignant at the insinuation that he'd done something underhanded. As he tried to defend himself, his testimony disintegrated: "I thought Mr. Malloy said he didn't want the pa...pa...PAPERS kept in his office..."

My poor Bren left the witness stand, crushed.

Des was questioned the next day. He appeared in the witness box in a distinguished pin-stripe suit, the very picture